TABLE OF CONTENTS

The Undertow	2
She Just Smiled	16
The Bench Maker	42
Cliffs	81
The Darkroom	94
Zero Man	111
The Fire on the Rock	132
#NoLivesMatter	142
The Last Rag	170
Shumana	202
The Tent in the Park	231
Naming My Tumors	254
Unblemished Sky	274

The Undertow

Almost every summer day of my youth was spent the same way. My mom, or one of my friend's moms, would drive us about five miles west to the spill way of the Pueblo Dam. It had been completed just a few years earlier to hold back the Arkansas River. I don't recall seeing a look of fear, or even concern, in any of our mom's faces. They just wanted to be left alone in the afternoon. It was the whole Luke and Laura era on "General Hospital".

That was 1979. When our moms dropped us off, we carried no canoe, no inner tubes, or life jackets. We sure the hell didn't wear any fucking helmets. It was just us in a pair of shorts and our shoes without socks. Chris would always wear baby blue canvas Chuck Taylor high tops. He squinted because he couldn't wear his thick glasses down the river. Eddy would always wear these white slip-on boat shoes that would come off in the rapids. I don't know how much time Chris and I spent sitting on the river bank while Eddy searched for a lost shoe. I would wear some white leather Adidas that had just got me through the school year.

We called it skiing down the river, letting the soles of our shoes slide across the slippery rocks. We got out and walked around the deep holes, even though we were all good swimmers. It gave us chance to let our skin unshrivel and soak up the sun. By the time September came around the three of us had skin darker than maple syrup. I'm sure that they had sunscreen back in those days, but I don't recall seeing it until at least a decade later. People didn't worry about every little thing back then like they do today.

Our favorite time of the year to be in the river was in late May to early June. That's when the snow melted off of the Rocky Mountains creating unruly whitewater down through Salida and out onto the eastern plains. Farming was still a thing back then. During that time of year, the water blasting out of the spill way of the dam was deafening. We could hear the sound a couple of miles down the river. It echoed through the limestone cliffs that lined the flowing watercourse. We eagerly jumped into the chaotic fluid that jerked and pushed us in any way that it wanted us to go. The rapid current imposed its will on almost all of our movements. On one of those instances where Eddy lost his shoe, the razor edge of a piece of limestone earned him eight stitches on his left heel.

Our journey down the river usually at the sharp bend, just before the river swept under the Pueblo Boulevard bridge and through a blighted downtown of the city. At the bend was a huge old cottonwood tree with a rope hanging over a deep hole. We would always take a few swings off the rope, competing to see who could do the best backflip of the day. I was prone to end the swing with a belly flop. Chris was prone to back busters. Beyond the cottonwood with the rope, across the railroad tracks, was the steep trail that led up to Goodnight Avenue where our homes were.

The best stretch of the river flowed below the bluff that our houses were built on was about two thirds of a mile upstream from the cottonwood tree. It was probably about 150-yard stretch. At the end of it was a big sandy beach, that after coming down from the dam we would lay on and soak up the blazing rays of the sun. Sometimes we would stash a joint in Band-Aid tin so we could get high after skiing down the river. Occasionally we would fish from that beach, but in a river known for its incredible trout all we ever caught there were suckers. There were times that we would set up tents and camp there. Of course, the prerequisite to those nights is talking Eddy's older sister into buying us a twelve pack of Miller High Life.

On the east end of the stretch was what we used to call the "slabs". It was just a pile of bricks some of which was still held together by mortar. Chris' grandpa told us one time that it used to be a big house that was destroyed in the big flood of 1921. Almost 1,500 Puebloans died between June 3rd and June 5th of that year. I remember when he told us that story that there were tears in his eyes. Chris' mom would tell us later that her dad had a brother and sister that were swept away in the flood waters. They never found the bodies.

Chris and Eddy didn't care much for that stretch of the river, but I loved it. To me, it was better than any amusement park. Between both banks, the water looked reasonably calm, but that was a colossal deception. While the two of them floated close to the south bank, I swam over to some small ripples on the north side. I would aim for a huge tree branch that hung mere inches above the water's surface. Just before it seemed like my forehead would slam into the bark, I would get violently jerked for what seemed like a mile underwater by a vicious undertow. The first time I got caught in it, I fought the force, and thinking that I was going to drown for sure, I gave up to my fate and just went limp. About fifteen yards later, the undertow would literally shoot you out of the water. I looked up at an unblemished sky. After that, I would float in with my arms crossed and allow myself to be sucked down. I tried to explain it to Chris and Eddy, but they weren't having it. They had both had a single experience in the undertow. That was enough for them.

It was around the Fourth of July in 1979, and I was walking into the driveway after having spent the day as usual at the river bottom. My mom literally sprinted out of the house towards me, "Johnny, oh my God, are you okay?" I thought that it was an odd question, and didn't know how to answer. As she hugged me, she asked again, "Johnny, are you okay?"

"Yes," I answered, both puzzled and annoyed.

"What about Chris and Eddy? Are they okay?" It was then that I noticed her slightly frantic tone.

"Yes. They went home. What's the matter?"

"Aunt Jenny called me, the police and fire department are looking for a kid that went underwater in the river and never came back up."

"We were at the rope all afternoon. I didn't hear anything."

"Thank god you're okay. I was so worried."

"How old was the kid?"

"They haven't said."

"Where did it happen?"

"Somewhere by City Park."

"Mom, you know we never go past the bridge. The water is too shallow and boring past that."

It turned out that it was a kid that I went to school with. It was after my freshman year of high school. It was a big school, so not only did I not know him, the name didn't even sound familiar to me. We looked up his picture in Eddy's yearbook, but Chris and Eddy didn't know him either. They searched the river as far as east as Avondale, but they didn't find a body. After a week, they gave up searching.

My family had just got back from a week-long road trip to South Dakota, where we did all the usual tourist attractions, like Mt. Rushmore, Deadwood and the Badlands. The day after we got back, Chris' mom was driving us out to the dam. It was late July by then, so the river was way down from where it had been in June. I told them my trip, and they told me about how bored they had been the past week. We talked about jobs we could do to earn money for the state fair in August. Eddy told us that there were people on the sandy beach, so he had to stash the Band-Aid tin with a couple of joints in it by the slabs.

As we sat there passing the joint around, I asked Eddy what kind of weed it was because it really stunk. Chris concurred. Eddy said he didn't know; it was just something that his sister had given him. After a while we were high enough that we didn't really care. We just wanted to get to the Loaf n' Jug to get some Fritos and bean dip.

The next day, we sat on the slabs again. This time we didn't have anything to smoke, but the smell was still there. I told them that it smelled like the time my hamster got out of its cage and got into the hall closet and died. The three of us got up and looked around. Eddy surmised that a beaver had probably got under the slabs and died.

Over the next few days, the smell got progressively worse. By the time Saturday came around we would get out at the water at the sandy beach and bypass the slabs because the smell was starting to make us gag. There was a trail that would lead us directly to the cottonwood with the rope. I was disappointed that I couldn't ride out the undertow. Chris and Eddy expressed no sympathy for me.

On Sunday morning, I was in the garage working on my motorcycle when my step-dad came up and showed me the newspaper. The headline read, "Missing Boy's Body Found". There was a photo of the slabs. A fisherman had called the police to say that that there was stench of death in that section of the river.

I got on my motorcycle and rode down to the slabs. I got off the bike and walked around for a bit. The smell was still there, but it was faint. I thought about what I had read in the article. The authorities said that they had not searched the area because the boy's friends and other witnesses said the boy went under about a mile and a half east of where the body was found. There wasn't a person quoted in the piece that could explain how he got upstream. His mom said that the boy was a good swimmer and had taken swimming lessons since the summer before he started kindergarten. The fire chief went so far as to say that it was likely to be a mystery that would never be solved.

As I sat on the old red bricks with the river flowing slowly by me, I looked over at the north bank. I could see the ripples flowing under the tree branch. Nobody else would understand it, but I knew exactly what happened. I don't know how he got out of the water downstream without being noticed, but like my friends and I, he wanted to take one last trip down the Arkansas before the sun went down. Across the river from the sandy beach was a path into the water. The kid went in right there, before he knew it, the undertow had him. He panicked. He exhausted all of his energy in the fight. Unlike me, he didn't resign himself to his ultimate fate. He just kept fighting. The undertow won and sent him to a watery tomb under the slabs.

Now, even as a middle-aged man, I think often about the lesson that the undertow taught me. Life is full of strange and sometimes dangerous currents, but if you just relax and enjoy the ride, everything will be alright in the end.

She Just Smiled

When Adelle and I started planning this cruise nine months ago, she said that if we couldn't get a suite, she wanted a room with an ocean view. I balked. "We may as well get the cheapest room, I only plan on being in there to sleep". It took a week of passive aggressive tension, before she finally relented and said that we could get an interior room. I told her that I would make it up to her in so many other ways. She just smiled.

Adelle had never wanted to do a far east cruise. She preferred the Mediterranean. I persisted. She offered up various alternatives. The Caribbean. I reminded her that we had already done that. She floated Alaska. I dug in, and told her that I sure as hell didn't want to take a cruise somewhere cold. She said that there was a nice cruise that would take us to England, Ireland, Scotland and Norway. Once again, I told her that those places seemed like very cold places.

For a week, she continued to suggest cruises other than the far east. She went to a travel agent and brought home several brochures. She was excited about one that went to South Africa, Australia and ended up in New Zealand. I told her that it was beyond our budget. She pulled another brochure from the stack. It went down the St. Lawrence River. I asked her once again why she wanted to go to a cold place. She stared blankly at me before starting to flip through the brochures again.

"How about if we just keep it simple," she said. "Here's one where we leave from San Diego, and it stops at all the major ports in Mexico. It won't get much warmer than that."

I opened the brochure, and feigned interest. "Have you read about Mexico lately?" I asked. "The cartels have completely taken over the country. Back in the day, they only killed themselves, but not anymore. Now they're killing innocent people including women and children. Just last week they even killed tourists in Cabo. Cabo used to be the safe place to go."

"Okay Don." She bowed her head and pushed the stack of brochures to the center of the table.

I pulled out some pages that I had printed off of the internet. "How about this," I said and handed them to her.

She looked at them and slightly rolled her eyes. "The far east? There are so many people there. You know how uncomfortable I get around that many people."

"It's not that way everywhere. We can find some remote places."

"Adelle, it's Thailand, Cambodia, Ho Chi Minh City, Singapore. It will be great."

"Don…"

"Adelle, you know how much this would mean to me. Ever since I found out that my biological father was killed in the Vietnam War, I have felt the need to be there. I want to feel what he felt in his final moments."

She just smiled. "Okay Don."

X   X   X   X   X   X   X   X   X

Now, as I sit here in this windowless room, strangely lit in a way that caused no shadows, I wished that I had listened to Adelle. I wish that I had listened when she said that she wanted a room with an ocean view. I wished that I would have listened when she said that she wanted to take a Mediterranean cruise. Actually, I really wished I would have listened when she said she wanted to go to South Africa, Australia and New Zealand. We could have afforded that, the Mediterranean cruise, the Alaska cruise, and probably had enough left over for the cruise that ended up in Norway. I wished I would have listened to her. I wish that I would have listened to her about everything.

Most of all, I wished that I would have listened to her about Ethan.

I guess that it has been right around two and half years ago that she came to me and said that she had found marijuana in our son's room. I literally laughed in her face. "What's the big deal? We've both smoked pot in our lives, it's no big deal. We both know that we have done way worse things. When we first started dating, we were snorting cocaine like we were Hoover vacuum cleaners."

"But Ethan is not like us..."

"Nonsense," I interrupted her. "Ethan is your normal, average, evryday high school kid. The world is different now than it was in the eighties. Technology has changed everything, but that doesn't mean that kids are any different. We grew out of it, and so will Ethan."

She just smiled.

About six months after that, right around Christmas, she told me that she had found something else in his room. "Jesus Christ Adelle," I raised my voice to her. "Why do you have to go snooping through Ethan's room? He's entitled to his privacy".

"Aren't you even going to ask what I found Don?"

I could feel my eyes roll. "What did you find Adelle?"

She held up a plastic bag with a few pills in it. "I looked them up. They're Oxycodone."

We confronted Ethan about the pills. He said that a friend had stolen them from his parent's medicine cabinet and given them to him. He said he had them for a few weeks, but hadn't taken any of them, he was too afraid. He had other friends who had taken some and overdosed and he didn't want to end up like that. I told him that he wouldn't be trying those. He agreed. I took the pills and put them down the garbage disposal. Then he said that he was going to go to the high school basketball game that night. I told him to be careful. We had had snow the day before, and the roads might be icy.

After he left, I could tell that something was bothering Adelle. "What is it?" I asked.

"What do you mean 'What is it?' Our son had a serious narcotic, and you treat it like it's nothing."

"It is nothing. It's just a phase. He'll get through it."

"No, Don, Oxycodone is something. It's a very dangerous something. We need to get him some help."

"Adelle, I promise you it is nothing."

She just smiled.

X   X   X   X   X   X   X   X

It was Valentine's Day morning, a Saturday. On New Year's Eve, Ethan had met a girl, Laney. Adelle didn't care for her, she thought she was too wild for him. I told her to relax. I thought she was perfect for our son. He needed something to get him away from the video games. Adelle liked it when Ethan played Fortnite all day. She knew that he was safe. I couldn't stand it. I thought he should be out of the house doing other things. When I was his age, I couldn't stand to be in the house. That might have been because my parents fought all day, every day. Adelle and I weren't like that. We rarely rose our voices to each other. She has always been a very agreeable woman.

Ethan had very big plans for the day. Laney was his first real girlfriend. The two of them were going to go snowboarding with some friends. That night he was going to take her to one of the nicer steakhouses in town. The night before he had gone out and bought a dozen long-stem roses, a heart-shaped box of chocolates, and a gigantic teddy bear. He was beaming when he showed us the gifts. I teased him about how he was trying too hard to get laid. Adelle just smiled.

I woke up that morning to the sound of the doorbell. It was Laney. "I've been trying to get ahold of Ethan. He hasn't been answering his phone."

"He's always sleeping through that damn phone alarm of his," I said. "I wish he would get an old-fashioned alarm clock. I'll go bang on his door."

Just as I said that, I heard Adelle scream and start crying. I ran up the stairs. Adelle was on her knees with her face between her arms, sobbing. I looked into our son's room. Ethan was face up on his bed. His skin was blue, and there was black shit coming out of his nose and mouth. There was a syringe still stuck in his arm.

X　　X　　X　　X　　X　　X　　X　　X

After Ethan died, I sold my financial planning business for a pretty decent sum. I couldn't concentrate on other people's needs and hopes. I had suddenly found the whole process to be mundane and pointless. I no longer cared whether anybody else had enough money to retire on. For a few months, I could barely get out of bed in the morning. When I was able to get out from under the blankets, I wouldn't shower or eat breakfast. I would just drive to my boy's grave and sit there for hours on end. It didn't matter what the weather was like, the only place I felt comfortable was six feet above where my son was.

Adelle had no such problems. Ethan's funeral was on a Friday, and she went back to her job as a pediatric nurse the next Monday. Her hours at work gradually got longer and longer until it got to the point where I was already in bed by the time she got home. On her days off, we might take a day road trip through the mountains. If we stayed at home, she would still be working, saying that she had paperwork to catch up on. I would read books or watch the History Channel. I liked learning about the Vietnam War.

One morning over coffee, I casually mentioned that I thought we should sell the house and go start over somewhere else. Adelle slammed her cup down on the table so hard that some of coffee hit the ceiling. I had only seen it once or twice in our 18 years of marriage, but there was absolute fury in her eyes. "How fucking dare you make such a suggestion! How fucking dare you! Do you think that you are the only one that misses Ethan? Just because you go to the cemetery every day, you are the only one that misses him? I will not leave this house, not now, not ever. I will die in this house just like he did. You might feel close to him when you are next to his grave, but when I am in his room, I can literally feel him. I know you don't like going in there, but his presence is still in that room. He is still in that room, and I will not leave him."

"I'm sorry. I won't bring it up again."

For the next week, Adelle must have been feeling guilty about blowing up on me. It was so out of character for her. She worked only eight-hour days, and made sure that we had dinner together every night. We would take turns cooking. I grilled steaks one night, she made lasagna the next. I made tacos, she made beef stroganoff. We held hands while we watched movies together. That week, for the first time in months, we made love.

On Sunday, we went to Ethan's grave together. She didn't like going there, just like I wasn't a big fan of going into his room so we didn't stay long. We drove into the mountains to a lodge famous for its brunch. We took the long way home just enjoy the scenery.

"Adelle?"

"Yes."

"Have you given any thought to quitting your job?"

"Why would you ask that?"

"Have you?"

"No, I haven't"

"Would you?"

"Where are you going with this Don?

"I need to get away."

"Where?"

"Anywhere. I guess this what I was feeling when I was

mentioned selling the house, and before you get angry, I

regret ever suggesting that."

"I don't know, I like my job."

"I know, I think a change of scenery would do me, us,

good."

"What do you mean, 'change of scenery?"

"We could travel. See the world. I know how

important your career is to you...."

"I love my job. I love the babies. I make good money."

"We don't need the money. We need each other."

Adelle didn't answer. I just kept driving. She stared

out the window,

Instead of cooking dinner that night we stopped by the store and picked up a tray of sausage, cheese and crackers. I told her to grab a couple of movies from Redbox, and I would meet her at the car after I grabbed a bottle of wine from the liquor store. She barely spoke until after we had a glass of wine and were about to start the movie.

"Don, what will happen if I don't quit my job?"

"I don't know, but I need a break from this place, this city, this life, I just need to get away. See the world."

"Would you go without me?"

"I haven't really thought about it."

"You could start another business."

"No."

"I love my job."

"I know you do."

"Don?"

"Yeah?"

"Will you leave me all alone if I don't quit my job?"

"Ugh….No. Of course not?"

"That doesn't give me confidence."

"I love you Adelle."

"Okay, I'll give my notice tomorrow."

I kissed her. "Thank you."

She just smiled.

The only condition that Adelle set for our travelling was that we be home at least one week per month, I readily accepted. She could spend time in Ethan's room, and I could be by has grave. The first trip was a roadie around the country. We took another one to Alaska. We flew to Europe, and to Brazil. We took cruises through Central America and to Hawaii.

Adelle never said if all of the traveling helped her grief. I guess it helped mine. As much as grief can be helped.

X   X   X   X   X   X   X   X

I guess that I am going to end up breaking my promise to Adelle. In three days, it will have been one month since we landed in landed in Tokyo to start this cruise. Although it wasn't Adelle's first choice for a cruise, I thought she seemed to be enjoying herself. Despite the throngs of people around her, I could tell that she really liked Hong Kong. I was surprised.

In hindsight, as I sit in this windowless room, I think that is where it all started. That night, while having dinner on the ship, Adelle pointed out a woman at the table next to us. "She does not look well." I looked over at the woman. She was pale, and there were beads of sweat on her forehead. It appeared that she was having trouble breathing. The man that she was with dipped his cloth napkin in a glass of water and dabbed the woman's face. I looked at my wife and nodded in agreement.

When we got to Ho Chi Minh City, I could barely contain my excitement. This was the whole reason I wanted to go on the cruise. I had this weird fantasy that I was going to feel some kind of spiritual connection to by biological father, even though my mom told me he was deep in the jungle when he stepped on a land mine. It was almost dusk when the ship pulled into port. I would have to wait until morning before I could go into the city.

I woke up in the middle of the night to Adelle coughing in her sleep. If she wasn't coughing, her breathing was short and labored. I felt her cheek. I didn't need a thermometer to know that she had a fever. As much as I wanted to let her sleep, I couldn't help but wake her up and ask her if she was okay. She was irritated, but said she was okay and went right back to sleep. I tried to go back to sleep myself, but the sound of her breathing wouldn't let me. I could feel the dampness on the sheets from her sweat.

The next morning. she was alert, and actually looked pretty well. She got up and took a shower and I only heard her cough a couple of times. Her breathing sounded fairly normal, just the occasional wheeze. When I gave her a hug, she was still a little warm, but not as hot to the touch as she was during the night. I asked her if she wanted to go get some breakfast before we went into the city. She asked if I would be upset if she skipped going into the city, and she asked if I would bring her back an English muffin and raspberry jelly before I left. She just wanted to spend the day relaxing. I told her that I thought that was a good idea and I would see her later in the afternoon.

I went into the city, but didn't see much of it. I spent

the entire day at the Bảo tàng chứng tích chiến tranh, or The

War Remnants Museum. There were numerous exhibits of

American war machinery, helicopters, planes, unexploded

ordinance, including land mines, and even the cages where

they kept the American prisoners of war. There were a few

times during the day, where I had tears in my eyes thinking

not only about what my father went through, but what

everybody, on both sides went through during that ridiculous

conflict.

I was emotionally spent as I boarded the ship that

afternoon. I hadn't eaten anything since breakfast and was

starving. I was hoping that after a day of relaxation that

Adelle would be feeling well enough to go to dinner. As I

walked up the dock, I noticed a group of soldiers at the

entrance of the boat. They noticed me too. They were

pointing in my direction.

As I stepped on to the deck, I was greeted by seven people all wearing medical masks. They were barking at me in Vietnamese. I shrugged my shoulders to let them know that I did not understand what they were saying. They motioned to a young lady to come over. I could see fear in her eyes as she put on a mask. Two of the soldiers put a mask on me. The young lady attempted to speak to me in English, but she must not have been a real translator. I was able to understand a few words, namely "quarantine".

The soldiers led me to my room. The doors to all of the other rooms were open, and they were all empty. Only the door to our room was closed. The soldiers motioned me to go in. I told them that I was hungry. One of the soldiers raised his gun slightly and motioned to the door. I nodded and went into the room.

Adelle was laying face up on the bed. She looked dramatically different than she had that morning. Her skin was grey, and her cheeks were sunken in. She looked like she had lost 25 pounds in seven hours. "Are you okay?"

Her response was labored, and she could only whisper. "There is some kind of virus."

"What virus?"

It seemed to take all of her energy to speak. "I don't know. We haven't seen the news. A virus started in China. Thousands of people have died. Hundreds of thousands more are sick. They think I have it."

I needed to speak to somebody. I need to know what was going on. The door to our room was locked from the outside. I started pounding and screaming. Adelle motioned for me stop. "It won't do any good. They aren't trying to harm us. They are just afraid."

As it turns out, those would be Adelle's last words. For the next two days, there would be a knock at the door around noon. It would be a single soldier in a hazmat suit with a pot of rice and a jug of water. There were no medical supplies, and that would be the only contact we had with the outside world. The ship had not moved in that time.

As Adelle deteriorated, a foul smell permeated the room. On the third day, with no warning, I started coughing. I could not stop it. It went on for the better part of an hour. When it was over, I couldn't breathe. It felt like there was a ping pong ball in my throat. The sweat rolling off of my head stung my eyes.

It was a snap decision. I sat down next to Adelle and felt her wrist. Blood was still pumping, but it seemed like forever between beats. I kissed her on her colorless lips, and said "Ethan misses you". I grabbed a pillow and put it over her face. There was very little struggle. When I pulled the pillow off, my wife had a little smile on her face.

I grabbed the sheet off of the bed and started twisting it up. I surveyed the shower rod. It looked like it would be strong enough.

The Bench Maker

I couldn't decide if ten years equaled a millennium, or just one second. I guess I should just be thankful that it happened in ten years. When the judge told me that he was sentencing me to twenty years, I wanted to cry but there was no way that I was going give to him, or the bitch sitting on the other side of the courtroom the satisfaction. But, fuck, twenty years? I had only been alive for nineteen. I said sorry like I was supposed to, then they led me away in handcuffs.

Prison sucked, don't get me wrong, but it wasn't as bad as I expected it to be. It was my first offense as an adult, and they considered me to be non-violent, so they sent me to a minimum-security facility. I did my time in the Rifle Correctional Center, outside a small town in Colorado, almost in the middle of the state. It is about the same elevation as Denver, around 5300 feet, but it's on the other side of the continental divide in a more mountainous area. There were nights in my cell when you could small the pine air and I would just imagine I was on a long camping trip.

There were other nights, really not all that often, that I would be angry for being in there. I didn't deserve to be there. That girl wanted it as bad I did. She had been talking about it all night as we drank shot after shot of tequila. The plan all along was to get drunk and fuck. We met at the bar across from my apartment, the place didn't card anybody. She asked me to take her back to my place.

I had a bottle of Jose Cuervo Gold, and as soon as we walked into my apartment, we did three shots each, one right after the other. We started kissing each other and feeling each other up. She undid my belt and shorts, and I pulled her shirt over her head and pulled the bra straps from her shoulders. Once naked, we made out and just played with each other. She put her hand on my chest and said that we should do one more shot of tequila. We were both already so drunk that we could barely walk to the kitchen. After we did our shots, I told her to go to the bedroom, and I would be in after I took a piss.

I walked into the bedroom she way lying across the bed in an "X", her limbs stretched out to all four corners. I crawled on top of her and put myself inside. I started moving her. I asked if she liked it, and if it felt good. She mumbled something. I tried to get her to get more into it, I guess she just liked it that way. She must have liked it because she was making these low moans.

When I woke up in the morning, she wasn't in the bed. I looked around the apartment but she was gone. Her bra was still on the living room floor. My head was pounding, and I thought I was going to puke, so I went back to bed. I slept there until 3:19 pm. That's what the clock said when the banging on my door came. I tried to ignore it, but once they said that they were police, I knew I had to get up.

My heart was pounding out of my chest as I let them in. They gave me the standard "we want to ask you some questions" line. I said sure. They asked me about the girl last night. I told them that I met a girl at the bar, and in my hangover and nervousness I couldn't remember her name. She had been hitting on me, so we came to came back to my place and had sex.

I didn't know why they were questioning me, so I asked if the girl was alright. One of the cops said that she should be out of the hospital, and I asked what had happened.

The other cop said that the girl had told them that I raped her. I tried pleading to them, but they put handcuffs on me and took me to the Jefferson County Jail. By the time I was in court two days later they had charged me with eight different counts with the possibility of 113 years in prison. They had a lot of evidence against me, so when it was all said and done, I agreed to plead guilty to two of the charges, and the most the judge could sentence me to was 25.

Probably the worst night of my prison life was the Sunday before I was released. I had a dream, or a nightmare, or, I can't really think of a word to describe it. It was so lifelike, it didn't feel like I was even still in this world, it was like I was in a different place and time. There, I was walking with a young boy, probably 12 years old, he was holding my hand. We were on a path in a wooded area. The was a river that followed the path when it wanted to. There was no color in this place, there was black and white, or spectrum shades of grey.

The boy walked me through a field to a huge fallen tree. It had to have been there for decades, all of the bark had long since fallen off and the wood was sun-bleached. It was a huge tree, with its dead roots still sticking up 9 feet in the air. It must have made quite a sound when it fell. The boy let go of my hand and pointed over to a place near the bottom of the toppled Cottonwood. As I walked, I could see that it was a body that I was coming too. I looked back and the boy was gone. Even in this dreamlike state, my heart was beating so violently I could feel it in my ear drums. I was standing above the body of the same little boy, his torso was mostly gone, ripped away by some sharp object.

I was still thinking about the dream, or whatever it was, as they opened the gates of the Rifle Correctional Facility. I was handed a box with my possessions in it and an envelope. The first thing I was supposed to do was go see a parole officer. In his office, he told me what resources that were available to ex-cons. I was told the rules of parole. He asked me what my plans were, I wasn't sure, probably go back to Denver and try to get a job.

His facial expression was perplexed. "I got an email that said you had living and job arrangements upon release", he said.

I was as surprised as he looked. "I don't know what you're talking about"

"You didn't make arrangements with some craftsman from Meeker for a job and a place to live?"

"No," I shook my head in disbelief. "Are you sure I'm the right person?"

"This guy asked for you by name"

"How? I don't know anybody who lives in Meeker"

"He knows you. And, he must like you, because I can't name a single prisoner that was offered a job paying $25 an hour and free quarters to live in. You don't have to take it, but if you if want to see what it's about, the guy already paid one of the guards to drive you up there. It was almost dusk as I got dropped off at an old corrugated steel warehouse on the west end of town.

As the guard's truck pulled out of the dirt parking lot, I stood staring at the building. The sun was setting through cracks in dark storm clouds behind it. I wasn't sure what I supposed to be doing. I walked over to the side of the building to see how big it really was. On the side was a double-wide trailer, and horse corrals behind it. On the front, was huge garage door, big enough to drive a semi-truck through. On the southwest corner was a walk-in door. I'd try knocking on it first, if there was no answer, I'd try the house. I wondered if this was some type of set-up.

The door was a couple of inches ajar, so instead of knocking, I peeked my head in and called "hello"

"Back here" a voice called out from the far corner of the shop.

As I followed the sound of the voice, I looked around me. The place was probably the size of a football field, with 30-foot ceilings. There was a second level to the back quarter of the shop. The place was filled with benches. They varied in sizes, some of the benches were long enough for a dozen people to sit on, some would only seat a single person. There were wooden benches, marble ones, wrought iron, lava rocks and some that I had no idea what they were made of. There wasn't one bench that looked like the other. Each one unique. The craftsmanship shown in the details of each one were exquisite.

"Are you from the prison?"

"Yes," we shook each other's hand. He was ruggedly handsome. V-shaped physique, veins bulging out of his biceps, and a full head of dark, long, curly hair. He wore a neatly trimmed mustache and had teeth that belonged in a toothpaste commercial. He came across as friendly.

"Good. I read about you. You seemed the perfect man to be my assistant"

"Why do you say that?"

"Just a hunch," he smiled. "Come on, I'll show you where you can put your stuff." He told me about the details of the job as we walked. "It starts out at $25 an hour, if you're doing a good job after thirty days, I'll kick it up to thirty. After six months, I'll throw in health benefits. You can use the shop truck anytime you want, unless you are using it to do something that would break your parole." We came to a door on the second floor, and he showed me where I would be living. It was a big, nicely furnished studio apartment. It had its own private bathroom, which is something I'd been dreaming about for ten long years. He showed me that the refrigerator and cabinets were stocked with food, and that if I didn't like what was there, then my first paycheck would come in a week. He told me to settle in, relax for a little bit, and then go downstairs to his office.

As I walked to the stairs, it occurred to me that the shop was remarkably clean. There was no clutter, no dust on the floor, all of the tools looked like they were supposed to be where they were. The office was equally in order, no papers scattered about, just a laptop sitting in the middle of the desk, two leather office chairs on either side. He told me to have a seat.

"As you've already figured out, I am a man who makes benches," he said with a warm, beaming smile. I could see in his eyes that he was truly happy, and loved what he did.

"I was noticing them as I walked in, they're beautiful. It never occurred to me that there could be such a demand for benches"

"The demand is so great, that I turn away more customers than I accept"

"Why don't you open another shop?"

"Because there is only one of me. Each one of those benches is made by my hands, from my vision. I can't hire people who will see my vision. I hired you, because this kind of work has taken its toll on my body after all these years. I started making them when I was 12 years old. My body doesn't react to it the way that it used to. I need somebody to do pre and post work. While I'm working on the benches, you ship the one I just finished and get the material ready for the next one. You'll be doing some cleaning too, but all in all it's a pretty easy job for the money. You'll have plenty of downtime, but don't worry, I'll still pay you for it. There's a nice trail behind the corrals, goes on for miles. If it were me that just got out of jail, hiking that trail would probably be the first thing that I did"

The man's lust for life was so refreshing. I wasn't sure if he had an angle of some kind, but he was hard not to like. Still, I was curious. "Is it just the super wealthy that order custom benches because they bought a new mansion?"

His face took a more serious tone. "Sometimes. I donate a lot of them. This has never been about money for me"

"This is a hobby? You're doing all of this for fun?"

"Yes, if that makes it easier for you to understand. I know that you haven't walked through a park in at least ten years, but before you went in, is that something you liked to do?"

"The was a park close by. It had a lake that I used to run around"

"Were there benches in those parks?"

"Yeah, there was probably a bench every fifty yards or so around the lake"

"Was there something unique about each bench?"

"No, they all looked the same to me"

"Think harder. There wasn't something that made them different from all of the others?"

"Now that you mention it, each one was donated in memory of somebody who died"

The man was smiling again, almost childlike. "That's what I do. That's what I specialize in. They are called in 'In Memoriam" benches. They are monuments to the lives of people who made some kind of impression on their fellow humans while they were alive"

"That's pretty cool," I said with a slight laugh. I could tell that his outlook on life might be infectious.

"Before I accept a customer, I get to know the life of the person that the bench is going to be dedicated to. I want to know who the fruit of my labor is going to be a tribute too. I know that sounds arrogant, many of the people that die will not be missed at all. I don't judge a person's life, the deceased need not have lived a perfect life, but somewhere, as I learn the story of their existence, I want to see that they made a difference. There are so many ways to make a difference in the world, many that you aren't even conscience of, and when you think about it, a positive difference versus a negative difference is just two sides of the same coin"

"How do you know?" I was fascinated by what he was saying. "How can you really know, if you never actually met the person?"

He pointed across the room. "You see that bench over on the work table?"

"Yeah"

"That bench is for Audina Rae Conley. September 8, 2016 – March 28, 2020. She was three years old. She was the first child to die of Covid-19. While everybody was saying that the virus only effected the old and the sick, she was the first child to die of it. Nobody contacted me about a bench for her, her family is extremely poor which is why she couldn't get the medical treatment she needed. I'm arranging to have a bench placed under a tree in park by her house. There are certain people that just deserve to be remembered. A simple bench is the least I can do in her memory"

The job was even easier that the guy said it would be, there was some heavy lifting to be done occasionally but that was the hardest part of it. I kept wondering why he even needed a helper, but I wasn't going to question it out loud. When he was working on a bench, the guy would explain to me what he was doing, never in a condescending way, he really wanted me to understand his art. He started going over the applications for benches with me. If there was nothing else to do, he would have me read news websites, and if I found any tale of a dead person with a good story, he wanted to know about it. True to his word, after one month he kicked me up to $30 an hour.

There was no clock in this man's world. If he decided to work, it didn't matter what time of the day or night it was. If I was awake, I would usually go down and ask him if needed help, sometimes he did, and sometimes he didn't. There were times that he got into a zone while he was working and I doubted he knew I was even there.

It was around three in the morning, that I heard him down in the office. I could tell that he was trying to be quiet, but I was a light sleeper. A curse and a blessing when you are in prison. As I walked down the stairs, I could see he was working at his laptop by a small lamp.

"Anything you need?"

He locked his hands behind his neck and leaned back in his chair. "Sorry I woke you up. Just because I can't sleep doesn't mean I should inflict the same on others"

"I wasn't really sleeping. A habit I picked up in the corrections center. I almost think I forgot how to sleep?"

"Do you drink?" He asked.

"I haven't had a drop since the night I was accused of raping that girl. That's not to say that I wouldn't drink, I just haven't had that many chances in the last ten years"

"How about a beer?"

"That sounds really good"

He handed me some type of beer I had never heard of, but it was good. "Maybe you can help me. While I'm gone, I'm want you to take a look at an application that I received. I can't decide whether I want to do a bench or not"

"Okay. Where you going?"

He looked at me quizzically, then smiled and rolled his eyes. "My apologies. Sometimes I get so wrapped up in my own little world. My wife lives in Mexico. Every two months I go and see her for a couple of weeks. Some people think it's an odd arrangement, but it works for us. In September it will be 34 years. Married her while I was on a trip the summer after I graduated from high school"

"That's a pretty cool story. How come she never moved here, or you there?"

"She tried to move here once. She loved it in the summer and fall, but wouldn't you know it, the year she was here we had the worst winter in fifty years, in January or February, the temperature never got above 10 degrees. That was enough for her. As for me going there, my grandfather started this bench thing, and handed it off to my father and down to me. This is where I belong"

"You two should write a book"

"Maybe someday, but the story isn't finished yet. Anyway, since I'm on vacation so are you. You have free run of the place. Go hiking. The fishing is great around here. Hey," his voice got suddenly excited, "why don't you take the truck to Denver and see your family?"

"Thank you. That's very cool of you"

He stood up from his chair, and tucked the laptop under his arm. "I just emailed you that application. We'll talk about it when I get back. Now get some sleep. In a few days, I'll have a better idea of when I'm coming back"

He was gone in the morning. It was a strange feeling. For the first time in over ten years, I could do anything that I wanted. I was under nobody's schedule. I drove to Denver to see my mom. She seemed less than enthusiastic to see me, but she was cordial. It was the same fake conversation that I had been having with her my entire life. I went and saw some friends, they pretended to be excited to see me, but I could tell that in the back of their minds they were thinking "rapist". What I had been planning as a weeklong stay lasted all of two nights.

As I was leaving my mom's neighborhood, something caught my eye, in a field was a fallen tree. I parked the car and started going towards the tree. As I walked, my body was buzzing, I could hear a hum in my ear. My heart was beating rapidly, and my breathing was heavy. A wave of darkness draped over me. The next thing I remember was driving west past the Red Rocks entrance on Interstate 70.

Since I was in no hurry, I would use the rest of the week to just drive around Colorado and see what had changed in the years of my incarceration. When I was a kid, I used to travel all over the state with my dad. He was a field representative for a bank that made trailer home loans. He had Colorado, Wyoming, and western Utah as his territory. When I was on summer break, he would take me on a couple of business trips. Even though he was working, he still made the trips fun for me, and we did so many cool things. When I was 11, my dad was driving a highway between Canon City and Colorado Springs when an oncoming dump truck blew a tire and hit him head on. He died instantly.

When I got back to my room at the shop, it was mid-morning. I had spent the night in Grand Junction, so it wasn't a far drive. As I lay on my bed, I felt different. The ex-con who left this room last week, was not the same man who returned. I felt like I had no past, yet it had me in its clutches for a reason that was too abstract for me to articulate.

That afternoon, I decided to hike the trail behind the horse corrals that the man had talked about so often. I had taken small treks in either direction a few times before, but with a lot of daylight left, I wanted to see if it had an end. Probably two to three miles into the hike, there was a sound distinct from the noise that was made by the wind blowing through the pines. I stopped and listened to the high pitch. It didn't sound like an animal or a bird, and the only thing that made sense was a scream. I hurried my pace, but couldn't tell what direction it was coming from.

When I rounded a sharp corner on the mountain, the landscape changed instantly. What had mostly been a shady jaunt through tall Firs and Pines, became what was a desert climate. It was almost as though the trail had become a boundary line for two separate worlds. The tall trees remained to the east of me, cactus, sand and scrub plants to the west. Up ahead on the trail was a figure walking towards me. Just when I could make out that it was a small person, maybe an older child, it took a sharp turn into the trees. I called out, but it kept walking. By the time I got there, there was nothing to be seen in the trees. I just assumed that it was probably some kid who had been warned by his parents not to go around strangers.

When I got back to the shop, I grabbed a beer and turned on the tv to watch the news. My phone rang, it was a call from the boss. We exchanged stories and niceties about our vacations. I told him about my trip, and he told me how his wife was even more beautiful today than she was 34 years ago. He said he would be home in 9 days and asked me if I had gone over the application for the bench yet. I told him I hadn't had the chance. He asked that I read it at least a few days before he got back. He wanted me to really think hard on it. I assured him that I would.

The applicant died of AIDS in December of 1999 at the age of 32. Seven years earlier he had been one of three prime suspects in the brutal murder of a 12-year-old boy. A witness had seen him with boy earlier in the night. The applicant was arrested immediately on an unrelated outstanding for misdemeanor marijuana possession. He eventually cooperated with the authorities and gave them hair, saliva, and blood samples to them into the investigation of the boy's homicide.

The cops tried their hardest to pin the murder on the applicant, but they had no evidence linking him to the crime. His two friends, the other suspects, went through the same protocol, but there was nothing that could connect them to the murder scene. The witness would later recant her story, citing that it was causing her severe mental anguish. Three years after the crime, the applicant was convicted of possessing child pornography. His defense was that he had bought a computer from a pawn shop and didn't know the images were there. There was a renewed emphasis on the investigation into the boy's death, yet again, there was still no evidence tying the three to it. Still, in the applicants remaining days, he was still referred to by the police and newspapers as the "prime suspect". It was his mother making a request for the bench. She wanted a place to sit when she visited the place where her son's ashes were scattered.

After reading the applicants story, I was puzzled as to why the man would even consider giving this guy a bench. It was ingrained in me in prison that anybody who hurts a child is the lowest form of life.

That night I had one of those experiences similar to one that I had the week before I got out of prison. I was on the part of the trail that was a dividing line between worlds. My hand was being held by a short person in a black hooded robe. The trees to the right of me were perfectly still, like they weren't even real. Just up to the left, smoke was rising out of the desert. It was right in front of a large fallen tree. Between the flames and the wood, a boy's body was motionless, blood still draining from the wounds. I woke up in my room on the second floor of the shop crying.

That was a nightly occurrence, or some variation of, until the man got back to work. Almost immediately as he saw me, he asked me if I had gone over the application. I told I had.

"What do you think?" he asked.

"I'm kind of surprised"

"Why is that?"

"Because he probably murdered a kid"

"I didn't see it that way at all"

"He was convicted of possessing child pornography"

The man nodded his head in agreement, "That is the troubling part"

"As I was reading it, I found it hard to believe you didn't automatically reject it"

"Well, the application came from the mother, and I also pay a little extra attention to those. As far as the child pornography charge goes, and I read the trial transcript, if I was juror I wouldn't have voted to convict. I thought it was possible the images could have been on the computer when he bought it from pawn shop. If anything, I think it might have been some type of a setup. It seemed like the cops were going to nail him for something, anything, to try and get him into confess the boy's death"

"You saw it different than I did"

"I'm going to allow his mother to buy a bench. Her offer is more than generous"

"What made you decide that?"

"A mother will always be a mother. It must be hard to bury a child. That was the main reason I'll agree to it. Also, I want a tribute to the falsely accused. That man had to live the rest of his life under the cloud of suspicion. He didn't kill that kid, wasn't even anywhere close. The cops knew it, but in such a high-profile case, the cops couldn't tell the press that they didn't have a clue who killed the boy"

"That makes sense to me. When do we start on it?

"I'll start drawing up plans this afternoon. In the meantime, I'm going to have you start on a bench for somebody else"

"You want me to build a bench?"

"I think you can handle it. We're going to use one of the benches we already have. The black and grey marble one right on the first aisle. You're just going to detail and engrave it. He had a small lift machine to get the bench onto a work table. Get the detail carving done first, then put the dates on the plate in front. Just take your time, that should take a week, maybe a week and half. If you need help, I'll just be across the shop. Think you can handle it?

"I'll do my best"

"Any questions?"

"What are the dates?

"Oh yeah," he said. He handed me a piece of paper with "1993-2005"

"That was a long time ago," I said mostly to myself.

"Not really, if you think hard about it"

As soon as I started polishing the marble to prepare for detailing, I could feel an attachment to it. The first couple of days I thought I was just feeling pride of craftsmanship for the bench, but an obsession was the next step. I worked on it slowly and meticulously, making sure the most minute detail was perfect. I told the man that it was going to take longer than expected. He came and inspected the work I had already done, "very nice," he sincerely complimented. "Take all of the time you need. He'll still be dead when you're finished"

The bench was never off of my mind. I set the alarm for midnight to that I could do more work on it. I was still having those dreamlike experiences nearly every night. The bench became the focal point of each vision. With each experience I had, in them, the bench would move closer and closer to the fallen tree, closer and closer to the mortally wounded body. I didn't cry any longer when I came out of those trances, but I was sad and ashamed.

The man inspected my work when I had finished what he had asked me to do. "I impressed," he said with a beaming smile. He turned, put his hands on my shoulders and looked me pupil to pupil. His big smile became, "I'm so proud. I knew I had the right one"

"Thanks," his gaze was intense and awkward. I was seeing a sinister look that I hadn't noticed before. In that moment, the man gave me goose bumps.

That night, I lay still on the bed with my head on the pillow. I looked up the ceiling. I concentrated on keeping my eyes open. I didn't want to go to sleep. I didn't want to have another one of those haunting experiences, but the future would come whether I wanted it to or not.

As I walked the trail, the figure that held my hand wasn't wearing a black hooded robe, it was an older boy wearing a white suit, even his bow tie was white. I recognized him. It was the same boy that was there the first time this happened to me before I got out of prison. He walked me to the bench and we sat down. We watched as the wounded boy at the base of the fallen tree gurgled blood out of his mouth. The boy got up to leave. He smiled at me with black teeth.

As I was watching the boy walk away, somebody sat down next to me. It was the bench maker. "Are you proud of your bench?"

"Yesterday I was. Now, not so much"

"When I got the request to build a bench as a monument to you, I politely declined, explaining that they I didn't build benches for people that were still alive. But the requestor persistent, he had well-dressed men come to come to my door, approach me in parking lots, and even call me from wife's phone number, insisting that a bench be made for you. Once I read the application, I came to an agreement with them. The bench would be made, I would be paid enough so that I would never have to build another bench if I didn't want it to. I stipulated the monument wasn't to you per se, but a monument to 'Secrets'. A monument to those that think they have got away with murder, which on the grand scope of things, never happens. Nobody gets away with murder"

"How'd they know. I never told a soul"

"The application that came in for you wasn't from this world. Are you a religious man?"

"I tried it for a while in prison, but it didn't feel right"

"I'm not a believer at all. But still, I think this application came from the devil himself"

"After my dad got killed, I would just have random fits of rage, for no reason at all. I would usually black out when I had them". I nodded towards the bleeding boy, "I was in a rage that night that killed him, but I was conscious of it all. When I snuck out of my window that night, I knew I was going to kill somebody. He just happened to be the first person I came across who was alone. Without a word, I just shoved a butcher knife into his chest. He fell to the ground and I kept stabbing him. I didn't know his name until I read it two days later in the paper"

The bench maker stood up and looked at me, but he didn't say anything.

"I kept having those violent fits of rage, but over time I came to manage them. I learned how make them my own little secrets. I never killed anybody else. Even as I felt in a blinding rage, I mastered the art of being charming through it all. That's how I got the girl to go back to my apartment. I knew what I was doing with the booze. I had every intention of raping that girl, I don't think she even remembers the depravity I treated her with. Oh, and before we leave, and I wake up from this, I wanted to let you know that I know I ruined that man's life for letting him remain under suspicion for a murder I committed. I'm glad his mom is getting a bench"

I was about to stand up from the bench I made. The man motioned me down with his hand. "You're not waking up from this one"

Cliffs

I can still remember the sensation of falling. Words to describe it are hard to find when explaining it to other people. When I talk, they can imagine what it feels like, but they can never understand it. Most people think that it would be seconds of terror, but the reality is that time seems to stop, "suspended animation", for lack of a better term. My life did not flash before my eyes. The landing never crossed my mind, in fact nothing crossed my mind. Looking back on those few moments all I really remember of the sensation is a deep blue sky. I don't remember fear at all. I vaguely recall a feeling of release.

The area I grew up in was a spiderweb of limestone cliffs, cut into the Earth by centuries of a big river and its tributaries forcing its way through them. There were so many fossils in that delicate stone, collecting them wasn't even a novelty once you hit a certain age. You still picked up the ones that were whole, and the detail was good. Broken fossils were a dime a dozen, and you just walked past them. If there wasn't anything else to do, most of the kids in the neighborhood would be at the cliffs. We each had our own story of coming up on a rattlesnake sunning itself on the white rock.

In the summer of 1980, I was 14 years old. I was a reckless kid. I had no fear. Like most teenage boys, I was insecure so I had to prove how tough I was. If YouTube had been around back then, I would have died very young. I would have been the first one getting filmed doing some ridiculously stupid and dangerous stunts. It would not have ended well.

My pubescent bravado got the best of me one day in late June. There was a path across the upper face of a cliff near my friend's house. It was probably 75 feet above the ground. We called the path "the mousewalk", it was 18 inches at its widest point, and it was a good 20 yards to the other side. I had made it across four times before, each time on my hands and knees. We had heard stories of other people walking the length of it, but my friends and I didn't know anybody personally that had done it. My teenage testosterone kicked in, and I announced that I would be the one to change all of that. My friends cheered me on.

I was about two thirds of the way across, coming up on the hardest part of the trail. There were three overhangs that needed to be navigated in 25 feet. I had to stand still and catch my breath after making it around the first two. What made the last one so difficult is that it sat on an inward turn. Not only did you have to get around the hanging shale, there was blind spot as to where the trail went. I was hugging the rocks, using my left foot to feel for the path. The overhang gave way. An explosion of limestone blasting me off the cliff.

For what seemed like hours, I felt suspended and a force from below was holding me up. Clouds so close I thought I could touch them. The sun shining on me in that perfect temperature. Something interrupted that bliss. I maneuvered in the air so that my feet would hit first. Hundreds of years of erosion had formed an angular slope at the base of the cliff. I managed to hit the softer dirt closest to the cliff then rolled down where it was a field of small broken shale that down with me. I finally came to a stop about five feet into a thicket of thorn bushes. My friends were at the top of the cliff screaming, asking if I was alright. I yelled back that I was. A hundred feet above me, the sky erupted in laughter.

I managed to hike back up the cliff, and to arrive to all of the jokes my friends had been planning for me. I laughed along with them. It wasn't until a couple of hours later, my body covered in tiny bloody streaks from the thorns, that my ankle was the size of a grapefruit. A trip to the emergency room confirmed that nothing was broken. When I could walk again, I was back exploring the cliffs, without a second thought, but I never did the mousewalk again.

Something happened as I hit middle-age. Slowly, a snail's pace at first, a fear of heights crept up on me. By the time I was 45, my fear of heights became acute, but not all types of heights, I could look out of the top of a skyscraper with no problem, or I could stand on top of a tall bridge as long as there was a railing. I just didn't like unrestrained heights, it was tough to climb a ladder, let alone be on the roof.

By the time that I was fifty, I was drinking heavily. If I wasn't working, there was a beer in my hand. I kept a cooler in the car. The alcohol made my fear of heights manifest into other fears. The only time I didn't feel fear was when I was in the bar or in my room with a case of beer. I often dreamt of that day that I fell.

Despite my heavy drinking, I still went to the gym daily, and ate a mostly healthy diet. I thought I was in good shape. Then one week, after nearly a month and half of binge drinking, I felt a pain on the right side of my stomach. I didn't think much of it, the pain was light and sporadic. The next week, on a Tuesday morning, the pain was much stronger. By that Friday, I realized that the pain increased a little with each beer. My belly was bloated, I couldn't button the shorts that I had been wearing only a few days earlier. Sunday morning, I woke up in severe pain, but grabbed a beer and started drinking through the pain. I did that all day until the pain was excruciating. Around 10 that night, I was out beer and the thought that I was dying kept going through my head. For a fleeting moment, I thought about dialing 9-1-1, but passed out instead.

Since I woke up the next morning, even though I wasn't expecting to, I decided that I couldn't live like that anymore. Every good party has to come to an end. I made my mind up that I wasn't going to buy beer that week. Not having alcohol in my system was the easy part of not drinking, the difficulties lie in filling up all of the idle time which in the past had been reserved for drunkenness. I spent the first day taking a lot of the short walks around the neighborhood. In the next few days, the walks got longer and longer, I would drive to lakes and walk around them. The pain in my side was subsiding, and my view of life became slightly optimistic.

By the following week, I decided to challenge myself to see how long I could go without drinking a beer. I also got tired of walking on concrete, and with so many nature trails around me, I would start hiking. With each subsequent day, I would search out a more difficult trail to wander. I was soon getting bored with the "easy" trails.

Friday afternoon, in a gentle rain, I started my first "moderate" hike. It was much steeper than any of the trails I had done before. It was two miles to the top, and another mile and half down the other side. I had to sit and rest a couple of times on my way to the top, but I made it. Going down would be a cinch. About half way down, the trail took a turn. I looked ahead the next fifty yards. The trail wasn't terribly narrow, but if you missed a step or stumbled, there was a steep embankment waiting for you. A fall probably wouldn't be fatal unless you hit your head on something, but there would probably be a few broken bones on the way down.

I looked back, it would be longer, but at least I knew there were no falling points. I looked forward to trail and hill below. Fuck it. If I fall, I fall. If I die, it's my time. Sometimes you have to move through the fear. I walked slowly, paying attention to every pebble on the path, trying hard not to look down, even though that was an impossible task. Before I knew it, I was on the other side surveying the trek I had just crossed. Experienced hikers probably would have laughed at me, but fuck them. I had faced one my greatest fears and was still standing.

In the next few weeks, I grew determined to not just face my fear, but to conquer it, to go back to that 14-year-old boy who wasn't afraid of anything. I had to go deeper into the mountains if I wanted to continue to push my limits. I started to ask other hikers about trails they had been on, there were a few stories that piqued my curiosity. It was a girl with an Australian accent that drew me a map, and told me that this was the trail that I was looking for.

The girl's directions were impeccable. With her guidance, I found myself at an elevation of 12,500 feet. I stared down a trail that bore a remarkable resemblance to the mousewalk, even though it was made out of granite. There were only two outcroppings that a hiker needed to get around, but at the bottom of this cliff was not a soft slope of dirt and small rocks. At the bottom of this cliff there were not just rocks, but big rocks, jagged rocks.

I tried to eschew the fear from my brain as I started the walk. I had a blind determination to get to the other side. I had promised myself a reward, if I got through this, I was going to go to the nearest bar and have a beer. Getting around the first overhang was much easier than I had anticipated. As I approached the next one, I was smiling and brimming with confidence. I hugged it the way I had the limestone one so many years earlier. I could feel my feet on the trail. Just one more fingerhole and that would be it. I reached for it. I thought my eyes were going to pop out of my skull, when my fingertips felt the moisture on the rock. It turns out that the sensation was exactly the same as it was when I was a kid. I could hear laughing from the top of the cliff.

The Darkroom

It's safe to say that I pretty much grew up in a dark room, amidst the chemical smell, under the safe lights. If I hadn't, I'm sure that I would have had virtually no relationship with my father. He was the chief photographer for a newspaper in Santa Fe, New Mexico. He also did freelance work for a couple of magazines that covered topics in the southwest area of the country.

Photography was his passion, if we weren't in the dark room discovering what creations the film had given us, we were driving through the mountains, across the desert, into the canyons or even the occasional ghost town. He didn't like all photography, even for his job the thought of doing a portrait made him sullen. He absolutely despised doing social events like birthday parties, saying "go buy a Kodak 110 disposable camera, the pictures will turn out just as shitty as any that I can take." I remember some of his close friends asking him to be a wedding photographer. He would smile and do it, and the end product would turn out great, but he hated every moment of it.

As child, I often wondered if my father spent so much time in the dark room to avoid my mother. She spent most of my youth in a dark room as well, but it was her bedroom where she would spend her time chain smoking Virginia Slims and drinking Riunite wine. On those rare occasions, that she was out of her room, she would be hostile and combative. I don't recall ever having an affectionate moment with my mother. I spent most of my time with my father, but I wouldn't say that he raised me, I did that on my own.

It never occurred to me to be anything else in life except a photographer. With the help of some of my father's connections, I was selling pictures before I graduated from high school. Unlike my father, I had no qualms about doing social events or portraits. I thought some of my best work was portraiture, I just needed to be imaginative about the setting and the pose of the subject. I tried to stay with black and white photos, but had very little objection to color. I did whatever the checkbook asked me to.

Being a photographer was the ideal vocation for a young man in his early twenties during the late 80's. I had a friend that was a drummer in a heavy metal band, and he easily persuaded me to go out on the road with them and visually chronicle their first national tour. They had a minor hit that allowed them to open for acts that had slightly bigger hits than they did. There were no big arenas or stadiums, mostly 3000 seat venues. We partied our asses off, and hung out with groupies until the sun was coming up. Like I said, a great gig for a younger man.

When the rock and roll life style got old, I went to work for a travel magazine whose main demographic was senior citizens. It was a shock to the system to go from sharing dingy hotel rooms with a slovenly band to staying in five-star resorts around the world, and most importantly doing it on somebody else's dime. Eventually, that got tiresome as well. One can only take so many photos of hotel rooms before they all start to look the same.

As much as working for a travel magazine grew tiresome, I can't deny that it was lucrative. There was money in the bank, but passion for the art of photography felt stained by pimping myself out for corporate hotel chains, I decided that I wanted to get back to my roots. I wanted to be that little boy who was in awe of what my dad was doing in the dark room. I believe that it was one of my uncles that gave me a box of old paperback books. The box had been well travelled, held together by three or four rolls of black electrical tape.

I was disinterested in most of the books. I thought Mickey Spillane's detective books were cheesy. At the time, I didn't care for the classics. I still hate Shakespeare to this day. There were some Herman Hesse books that I liked, but it was John Steinbeck's "The Winter of Our Discontent" that made the biggest impression on me. I read all of his books, and each and every one of them made me wish I had the talent to be writer. The problem was, I lacked any type of cognitive abilities for writing. After all, I was a photographer. I could tell a story with a camera, not with a typewriter.

The last of Steinbeck's books that I read was "Travels with Charley". I don't want to overly simplify the book, because it is anything but simple, but the author writes about taking a road trip around America accompanied by his poodle Charley. Steinbeck wanted to capture the essence of the country at the time. I decided that I would try to mimic the journey, capturing the country through the lenses of various cameras that I stored in a large Sterilite container.

I bought a used Toyota Landcruiser and set off on my journey. On a side note, unlike John Steinbeck, there was no fucking way I was traveling around the country with a dog. I simply lack the patience for that type of thing. I tried to stay off interstates, sticking to the backroads. After almost four months of my journey, I captured some great shots and met some interesting people. But, since I am fairly foolish in financial dealings, the money I had saved came nowhere close to lasting as long as I thought it would. Dive bars and strip clubs have a tendency to chew a wallet up.

With my life's net worth dwindling down to three figures, except for the Landcruiser and my photography equipment, I accepted an offer to take up residence at a distant cousin's vacant property in Davenport, Iowa, which sits on the banks of the Mississippi River. He said that the basement would make for a great darkroom, and that I would only need to pay for utilities. I could sell some pictures and easily afford that, but winter was harsh, and there must be a million other of places that I would rather have been.

Davenport was a historical city, and it turned out to be a place that the camera loved. I captured some of the best shots of my career in that city. There is a festival in January of each year called "Bald Eagle Days". The birds congregated there as the river freezes and they search for food. Wildlife photography can be an absolute crapshoot, but out of nearly two thousand frames that I shot, one of them was truly a masterpiece. A bird magazine paid me a great sum of money for it. I could finally resume my road trip, and work my way back home, even though I didn't know where "home" was anymore.

With the check from the magazine in the bank, I decided to celebrate the only way I knew how, day drinking in shithole bars until the strip clubs opened up. I ended up a place called Déjà vu. Most of the girls, although they had nice bodies, would be dead before long. Some of them missing teeth because of smoking drugs, and if there were any left in their mouths, they were black and broken. There were other girls who had bruises about their bodies left by needles.

There was one girl though, who could only have been 18 or 19, that looked fresh and unused up by the world. She didn't have a single tattoo. She looked like she should be pledging a sorority come the fall, but here she was in nothing but a G-string dancing on a picnic table. I was surprised that none of the other patrons paid any attention to her. I think they knew that they wouldn't be able to fuck her by just showing her a baggy of meth. I showed her a $50 dollar bill, and asked for a private dance.

As we walked into a stinky room that was nothing more than sheet metal and two by fours, she told me that her name was Odyssey, and asked me what I wanted. I asked why she chose that name, she said, "you ought to see". As she danced, I asked her what attracted her to the lifestyle. She told me she was saving money to move to Los Angeles to become a model and actress. I didn't laugh, but told her I was photographer. I felt guilty for saying that, because I knew she would ask me to help with her portfolio. She did. It was the classic photographer trap that no girl could resist.

In the basement, as I set up a backdrop, and other props, for the type of photo shoot she wanted, she told me that her real name was Nikki, but she went by Nik as well. It was short for Nicolette. Still remembering how my father hated doing portraits, I wasn't sure how I was going to pose my subject. I could tell she was nervous too. She told me she had some clothes she wanted to wear, and asked me where she could change. There were only two doors, one was a bedroom, the other was the bathroom. I told her she could pick whichever she preferred.

It took her nearly a half an hour before she emerged from the bathroom. She was wearing a floor length, tight fitting, black silk sleeveless gown. There was a look of confidence on her face that I hadn't noticed before. I don't know, maybe it was something else. She just looked different. I wondered silently if this was the same girl that I had seen dancing on the picnic table. I couldn't reconcile the two images in my mind.

Few words were spoken as I photographed her, I didn't need to give her any instruction at all. It was like she had been practicing poses all of her life. The movement was fluid, yet precise. I was hoping the camera was capturing what my eyes were seeing. Then she stopped moving. She just stared at me. The camera kept clicking, but she was just standing still. She took her right arm and slipped the left strap of her gown off, and did the same to the other side. The top half of her gown hung at her hips. She used her thumbs to push the rest of the gown off.

I asked her if I should still be taking pictures. She walked slowly over to me and pushed the camera to the side. She used so much force to grab my crotch that it was borderline painful. She rubbed and rubbed and started kissing my neck before I even had a thought of reciprocating. When I did, the intensity seemed almost violent. Under the photography lights, sweat was running off our bodies like waterfalls. Her ass was tight. The whole act was brief, but it had passion of an entire night.

As we lay there recovering, she asked how long it would take to the develop the film. I told her I could have them done in about an hour. She asked why so long. I told her that the chemicals needed to do their thing. I could tell by her look that she wanted me to start the process. When I came back from putting the film in the tanks, I lay down next to her, and we started playing with each other again. The pace was slower, and gentler, but the passion was the same. After we came together, and caught our breath she asked me if I thought the film was ready. I thought the question was odd, but I told her that it probably was. She wanted to go look at the pictures.

I cut the film into sections, and put them in proof sheets. She stood off in the corner and just watched me in the dark room. I placed the proof sheets on the glass box with a florescent light inside. I started glancing over the negatives. I asked her if she wanted to look at them with me. She told he that she wanted me to describe them to her. I grabbed a magnifying glass and started going over them. With my face to the light, I felt a wave of darkness come over me. I thought that maybe I put the wrong proof sheets on the box, but there was no way that mistake could have been made.

I looked over to the corner, but said nothing. The voice asked what they looked like. I looked back down at photos. It made no sense to me. Every single image the same, hundreds of them. Again, Nik's voice asked what they looked like.

I said the picture was of a man. A naked man. A naked man with an erect penis. The voice seemed deeper when it asked me describe them. I said the face is yours, but the body is that a young man. All in all, very handsome. I started to ask a question but the voice asked me what else would I be expecting.

I walked over to the corner at stared at what I saw. The camera caught the right image. I guess it wasn't seeing what my eyes were. Again, I began to question, but he came over and embraced me putting his head on my chest. He asked me if I had felt the passion of the night in my veins. I couldn't lie, I had. He asked why it mattered then.

Zero Man

As I hiked up the mountain, the scene played over and over in my head. The door getting kicked open so hard, that the doorknob put a hole in the wall. Her face contorted as she lunged at me. Me pulling the covers over my head to protect myself while simultaneously pushing the neighbor girl off the side of the bed. The sheets being ripped a way and four of my wife's fingers in a claw-like position, her nails ripping four rows of flesh from my forehead down to my chin. The feeling of blood running into my eyeball.

A scream, an ear drum piercing scream. The sight of my wife holding the naked neighbor by her throat. I remember hearing yelling, but I don't remember what the words were. My four-year-old little girl in the doorway crying hysterically. The sounds of slaps. The sight of something flying through the air towards me. Paramedics shining a light in my eyes. A cop telling me that he needed to ask me some questions. Then my brain would replay it for me again. And again.

I had started hiking before the sun came up. I didn't want to dig my phone out of my backpack to know for sure, but I guessed it was almost noon. I found a rock in the shade and sat down a break. I thought about how I knew I had to get out of town. My wife was arrested for domestic violence against me, which automatically means a five-day restraining order. I told her that she could stay at the house, and I would go camping for a week. I picked a place in northern New Mexico that I knew wouldn't have phone service.

Even though I feel a lot of guilt for what I did, and I could feel the sweat dripping into the four scabs running down my face as I climbed, and that my kid saw it all, there were times when I couldn't help but laugh at the whole situation. Never in my wildest imagination did I believe that I could fuck my life up so badly. The neighbor girl was 17, over the age of consent, so nothing happened to me criminally, still I was always going to be known as the old pervert that fucked the high school senior. There was no doubt that my wife was going to divorce me, and I'm sure her brothers would love to kick my ass. She would get everything, and I hate to admit that she deserved it.

My wife was a good woman. We had met our freshman year at college, and there was an instant bond. We moved in together before our sophomore year. After we graduated, we spent a year living in Australia. We spent our twenties doing what most people do at the age, work when you have to and party the rest of the time. Stereotypically, when we turned thirty, she wanted to settle down and start a family. I countered that thirty was just a number, there was nothing magical about it. We would have plenty of time for a family later. We were married the next year. For a couple of months, we kept living just as we had in our twenties. We started looking for a house, even though I pleaded that buying a house was like a prison, we would be trapped. We bought a house two months later.

Instead of going out, we started having friends over for dinner. Instead of drinking beer and liquor, we started drinking wine. It seemed so disingenuous. The two of us went from being best friends to husband and wife, and then after our daughter was born, even that was gone, we were now mommy and daddy. I missed my old life.

Two months ago, I was sitting on the back patio watching ESPN and listening to some kids play in the pool next door. Something flew over their fence and into my yard. There was a knock at the gate, I said to come get whatever it was. The next-door neighbor's daughter walked through and I almost dropped my wine glass. She was flawless. Long blonde hair over tanned skin, and the perfect body, legs that went right up to her neck, something out of a suntan lotion commercial. After she picked the thing up, she came over and apologized. I told her it was no problem. She looked at the tv and asked what the score in the baseball game was. We made small talk about sports while I shifted my eyes back and forth so it wouldn't seem like I was staring at her body, but she knew. She asked me what I was doing at midnight. I laughed and told her that I would probably be sleeping. She told me that I should look out my window into her pool. Everything could have ended at that point. I could have just said "no".

I told my wife that I couldn't sleep and was going into the other room to watch tv. I put a chair by the window. At exactly 12 o'clock the neighbor girl walked nude down the steps of the pool and into the water. She kept looking up at our house as she rubbed the water over her body. She knew I was watching, and motioned into the darkness for me to come down. My life would be so much different if I just shut the curtains right then and there. Instead, I put a robe on and went down to the neighbor's pool. This started almost two months of near daily sex with the neighbor girl. The first month we tried to be discreet about our encounters, but in the second month we discovered that the sex was even more intense if there was a fear of getting caught. We started taking risks, which led to my bedroom door getting kicked so hard that the doorknob went through the wall.

I was getting tired and the sun was well on its arc down in the western sky. I could hear a vehicle in the distance, and when I am camping, I like to be as far away from the human race as possible, but all the sound meant was that there was a road nearby. It surprised me, I thought I had climbed above where vehicles could go, but this was my first time in this particular wilderness, so I didn't know for certain what was around. I found a flat clearing not too far off the trail. I took my backpack off and used it as a head rest for a while as I recovered from the ascent.

There was still some daylight left after the tent was set up, and enough wood for a fire had been gathered. I took a sip of off one of the two bottles of Crown Royal that I brought, and I went and walked through the forest to see if anybody or anything was around. I realized that it was a good thing that I sat up camp where I did, because about 200 yards to the west was a deep gorge. There was no way that I would have been able to navigate it until the morning.

I walked south along the rim of the gorge. There was a lone dog barking. I looked around and the best that I could figure out, it came from the hill right above me. I couldn't see anything. I hadn't brought a lantern on my walk, so I went back to the tent and made a fire. I ate some freeze-dried food that turned out to be delicious. I continued to sip from the bottle as the number of stars in the sky grew exponentially. You don't really comprehend how many stars there are if you live in the city. Night time in a secluded spot in the mountains has way of humbling you. As you look at the light show in the sky you experience how insignificant you really are. I know that's a cliché, but it's true.

I heard the dog again. This time it wasn't a bark, it was more like a yelp, like its paw got stepped on or something. I listened hard and I thought I heard a man's voice, very faint. The dog let off a string of barks, and I was pretty sure that I heard laughter. I was a little disappointed that there was civilization so close to me. It shouldn't be too bad if it's just a man and his dog. As I meditated about the tattered wreckage of my life, I started hearing voices, mixed in with some strange high-pitched noise. My phone said it was 9:45, I was annoyed, but I would give it 15 minutes before yelling something.

Before the deadline I set was even half over, not only did the voices get louder, a bright light was illuminating the top of the hill. I was irritated as fuck. I yelled to turn it down a couple of times, even on the slight chance I was heard. The thought crossed my mind to climb the hill and punch somebody in the mouth, but in my current situation, the last thing that I needed was an assault charge.

It didn't last long. Soon, the volume of the voices was dropped and light dimmed. I could live with it in my whiskey state as I watched the flames dance in the circle of rocks. My daze was interrupted by the sound of something coming through the trees. I jumped up and just walked in circles around the campfire until I found the axe. I held it across my chest as I watched a figure with a flashlight emerge from the forest. A man's voice asked who I was. I repeated the same question to him.

The man came closer and shined the flashlight in my face. I shifted the axe in my hand to a more ready position. "I asked who you were," he said.

"And I asked who the fuck you were"

"Are you one of them?"

"One of who?"

"Don't play games with me. How did you find me? Who sent you?"

"What in the fuck are you talking about? I'm was just minding my own business until you started making all that noise and filling the sky with that goddamn spotlight or whatever it is"

The man walked closer to me until I could see his face by the light of the fire. He was tall and slender. Bald on the dome of his head, but the hair that was left above his ears stuck straight out. He didn't appear to have a weapon on him, so I relaxed the grip on my axe. "What are you doing up here?

"I don't see how that's any of your mother fucking business, but if you look around you, you could probably figure out that I'm camping. Now, let me ask you, why the fuck are you bothering me?"

He gave a slight smile, "a man like me can't be too careful"

Sometimes I can't help but be sarcastic, "what kind of man are you?"

"I'm a man who exposes the truth. That makes me a very dangerous man"

I should have been telling him to go back up the hill, and leave me the hell alone, but I played along. "The truth about what?"

"HTWW"

"HTWW?"

"How the world works. PTB"

"Just talk normal. I don't feel like playing acronym games with you. What is PTB?"

"The powers that be"

"Look, just tell me what you're talking about. I don't want to play guessing games with you"

"The powers that be control the way the world works. They do this with NLP, uh, Neuro Linguistic Programming. Mind control. They indoctrinate your brain to make you a cog in their machine to control every last thing in this world. They won't be satisfied until they have absolute control over all humans. In the not too distant future, all newborns will be microchipped, so they will have work backward and track down all of us that don't have a chip and install one"

My initial reaction was to laugh, but I suppressed it. For some reason I wanted hear what he had to say. I asked him if he wanted a sip of whiskey. The question made him look around nervously, as if there were people in the trees. He looked at me studiously and said he would like a sip. I rolled up a log near the fire for him so sit on then passed him the Crown Royal.

He looked at the bottle in his hands, "the good stuff." After he took the sip, he nodded at me appreciatively.

"I would like to say that I am informed. Why do you say indoctrinated?"

"I'll bet your memories are manufactured by the powers that be. I'll bet your mind is filled with cultural falsehoods. The Apollo missions. JFK. 9/11. Gulf of Tonkin, The Manson…."

I interrupted him, "so, you're a conspiracy theorist?"

He was clearly annoyed by the question. "No, I'm not a conspiracy theorist. I see the truth. Flat earthers. Those people are conspiracy theorists. Bunch of fucking nuts if you ask me. The Earth is clearly round"

"Do you come camping up here often?"

"I'm not camping. I'm working. My job requires that I travel quite frequently. I live on the road. If I stop moving, I'm a dead man. But, to answer your question, I come here a couple of times a year"

"Tell me again, what kind of work you do you do"

"I spread the truth. I try to warn people what is coming."

"You get paid to do this?"

"I have a blog with quite a few subscribers. Some of them finance me on my quest, as they are searching for the same thing. They PayPal me donations. I also have some books and DVDs that I sell on my website"

"You're an author?"

"Yep. And a screenwriter. A documentary film maker. Any medium I can hijack to get humans to open their damn eyes"

"Have you done anything I might have heard of?"

"Probably not. My biggest selling book was called 'Planet Zero'. The film rights to it keep getting sold back and forth to different characters in Hollywood, but nothing ever happens, I doubt there's even a script. I regret selling the rights. Either Sean Penn or John Cusack has it now"

"Why is that"

"I hate Hollywood. They are a big part of the grand lie most people live. They are an influential faction of the powers that be. They create the cognitive dissonance. When I saw what was behind the curtain, the pedophilia, the Satan worshipping, the mind control. I didn't want to be a part of that. I wanted people to see what was really happening"

"How do they do the mind control?"

"The ways are countless. The media, especially social media. Vaccinations. Algorithms. Government propaganda. I could go on and on. They always try to frame it as debate, but their great power is division. The people that fight amongst themselves are already under their control. There are the few that like me. We see things clearly. We are the true enemies of the PTB. That's why they are always looking for us"

"I still don't understand who 'they' is?"

"Controlled operatives. They are the lowest level of the powers that be. They can be anybody. The young boy serving you your burger at McDonalds. Almost all the cops and firemen and medical personal. The pilot of your plane. Hell, it can be the little girl next door"

"What the hell did you just say?" His last phrase almost knocked the wind out of me.

"I meant that anybody could be a controlled operative"

"Sorry, I was thinking of something else"

I motioned the bottle to him and asked if he wanted last sip, because I was tired and had a long hike ahead of me in the morning. He took a swig and thanked me and told me to be safe on my travels. I wished him the same.

As he walked back toward the tree line he turned around, "Hey, I've been avoiding any kind of news the past couple of months, are there still all of those restrictions because of the coronavirus"

"There's some. You have to wear a mask almost everywhere."

He shook his head, "classic black op. They tried the same thing back in 2009. They would have had us all microchipped by now, except some peon in lab ran a test that he wasn't supposed to and saw what was happening. They had to scrap the entire operation"

"I have to admit, there's something about the whole pandemic that hasn't added up for me"

He whispered, "don't say that too loud", then giggled. "Covid-19 is just one of the fabricated social disturbances that the powers that be have working right now. The cop kneeling on the black guy's neck? That was all filmed on a sound stage in Hollywood. It creates the exact division that they want. Climate change? That was meant only to instill fear. The fact that the virus hasn't added up for you tells me that you suspect there is deception from the government, the media, or whoever, but I can certainly assure you that the deception is far greater than your imagination could comprehend. Absolutely nothing is as is it seems"

With that, he thanked me again for the Crown Royal, and I watched as his flashlight went through the trees and up the hill. The dog was barking in anticipation of his master's return. I stirred the fire until it was only glowing embers, then went to the tent and crawled into my sleeping bag.

I kept hearing the man's phrases, "the girl next door could be a controlled operative" and "nothing is as it seems" in my head. There, in the dark, I hated that the man had put the idea in my head. Did my wife approach the girl next door about seducing me? Did she have the perfect plan to divorce me and take me for everything? The more I thought about it as I slipped into a drunken sleep, the scenario seemed plausible to me.

The next morning as I putting all of the camping gear into my backpack, I kept thinking about my wife and the girl. It even crossed my mind to go back into town and confront the girl. As I hiked, I eventually made up my mind that I would keep my suspicions to myself. I wouldn't say anything. I didn't want to be labeled a conspiracy theorist.

The Fire on the Rock

My grandfather was a pretty spry old guy. He could climb up the rocks almost as well as I could, and he was doing it with a heavy back pack. He hated be calling "grandpa", and I couldn't blame him, he wasn't that old. He was only 16 when he got my grandma pregnant with my father. Grandma once told me that my grandfather wanted to have some kind of legacy if he didn't come back from Vietnam. I'm not sure what my dad's excuse was for getting my mom pregnant with me when he was only 15. I was just told that I was the product of an era.

I was mostly raised by my grandfather. My dad would pop in every now and then when he was traveling through. He would send me a birthday card every year, and they never had stamps on them because he would just use grandpa's address in the return area. He used to tell us that he was in a band that was just on the verge of making it big. The only difference now is that he has an actual job at a machine shop. I'm told that my mom tried really hard to be a mother for a few months, but it was something that she was never meant to be. She hasn't been heard from years, and nobody has a clue if she is alive or dead. She might be at a commune in Oregon.

My grandpa would always say, "you gave me life". He's been telling me that since I was little, but I didn't think too much about it until just a couple of years ago. We were where we are now, at the family ranch that somebody homesteaded sometime in the 1800's.

"Grandpa," I said to him as I watched the flames reflect of off his face, "How come you always tell me, 'you gave me life?"

"Quit calling me 'grandpa'. Until, you came along, I was dead. I got killed in the war."

I laughed a little bit but he quickly gave me a look to let me know that he wasn't kidding, and that what he was saying was no laughing matter. "It wasn't just you", he continued, it was grandma too, God rest her soul"

"What do you mean Grandpa?" He's the one that taught me to be an asshole.

"I saw so much death in those jungles, not just our side, but their side too. There were bodies everywhere. I looked at all of them. I couldn't help but look at a body that I came across. I studied them. They were all kids, just like I was a kid back then. I died a little bit with every one of them. By the time I got back to the states, there wasn't any life left in me"

My grandpa could always lose me with his words. Most of the time, my he rarely spoke. He had always done what a man was supposed to do, he got up, went to work, came home, ate the dinner that grandma had prepared for him. Then he would sit in front of the TV for three hours having a Seagram's and 7-up at the top of each hour. He never had more than three drinks.

After my grandma died of cancer a couple of years ago, I tried to learn how to cook so that grandpa would have something to eat. I could tell that he appreciated what I was trying to do, but there were a lot of nights we would just end up going to McDonald's or Burger King.

My grandpa would usually tell me stories when we were around a fire. He was always honest with me, maybe too honest for a child. Some of the things he said would give me nightmares. That night at the ranch he wasn't very talkative. When we were packing up the truck with the camping gear, I asked him what was in the brown leather bag that he was carrying, but either he didn't hear me or he just ignored the question. I let it go.

That night though, whether my grandfather knew it or not, that bag was like the elephant in the room. Most times that we are at the ranch, we would set up camp at the base of the rocks, near the cabin. It was a rare occasion that we climbed to the fire ring at the top of the rocks. The bag looked heavy as we climbed. There were even times that grandpa had to stop and catch his breath. I don't know why I didn't ask him again what he was carrying, it just didn't seem right.

Grandpa stood up and went over to the ledge of the rock. His eyes gazed over the endless horizon of forest, then he turned and looked at me. "Did you know that I haven't been to a doctor since I got home from the war?"

"Why not grandpa?

"I don't know. I've just never felt there was a good reason. I've always felt fine. There is no good that can come from going to a doctor. You can only get bad news"

"They could find something wrong with you that you didn't know about. They could save your life"

"I've told you a million times, you did that already"

Grandpa grabbed the leather bag from next to the rocks holding back the fire. He just stared at it, as he grabbed a beer out of his backpack and sat down. I was nervous to ask, but did it anyway. "Grandpa, what's in the bag?"

"I heard you when you asked me that earlier today. And quit calling me 'grandpa"

"Is it a secret?

He looked down at the bag, then over at me. "I guess. In some ways it's not a secret at all. In other's it's the biggest secret of all. That's why I brought it with me.

My grandpa was doing it again, saying things that I had to stop and think about. I think it was a trick to shut me up.

"They're journals"

"What kind of journals?

"Journals that I have written over the course of my life. I brought them up here to burn them"

"Why do you want to burn them? Are they about bad things?" I asked.

I could tell by looking at him that he was really thinking about the answer. "There were times that I wrote when bad things happened, but I wouldn't say that that is what they are 'about". I also wrote about all of the wonderful things happened to me. Some people think that I have had a hard life, but that's not true"

"You shouldn't burn them"

"Why is that?"

"I want to read them"

"And, that is exactly why I am burning them"

"Don't you want people to know you?"

"People do know me. You know me. Your father knows me. Grandma, god rest her soul, knew me better than anyone, knew me better than I know myself"

"I could know you better. I want to know about you when you were my age. I want to read about what you did in the war"

As soon as it came out of my mouth, I knew that I shouldn't have said that last part. He was angry. My grandfather always got quiet when he was pissed off. He unzipped the leather bag and through the first composition book into the flames. When it was sufficiently burning, he threw the second one on. He kept repeating the process, arranging the books in the circle of rocks so as not to choke the fire out.

After he threw the last one on, he looked at me said, "I didn't write those for other people to read. I wrote them so I could get the thoughts out of my head. I didn't want to think that that way anymore. I was young, I thought that if they were on paper, they wouldn't be in my head anymore"

"Why didn't you just tell somebody?"

"I told grandma. She held me when I cried. But she couldn't truly understand it. If you didn't experience it, you couldn't understand it"

"I guess, but I wish I could"

He reached in the bag one last time, pulled out another composition book and handed it to me. The pages were blank. He gave me a pen from his shirt pocket. "As long as we are around this campfire, you can ask me anything. You can start your own journal to burn someday"

#NoLivesMatter

I had been hit in the head with a metal chair several times before, too many to count. The correct way to hit somebody with a chair is to use that indention where somebody's ass goes, and then hit guy in the front of the forehead and use only enough force to put a slight dent in the chair. If the whole thing was going to be televised, you would then put the chair in a good position where the camera could get a closeup of it.

If you were friendly with the guy that you were in the ring with, it wasn't a big deal, part of the business, and there was little if no pain. If there was any pain, it would be gone after the two of you had a few drinks at the bar next to the motel. You would talk about what was good in the match, and what didn't work. After that, you'd bounce ideas off of each other about how to make the next nights match even better.

Like I said, that's how it goes if you are friends with the guy you are working with. But, if you and the guy you are working with genuinely don't like each other, the match could go in a different direction, and things could get messy. That's what happened to me on the night of May 5th, 1995 in Las Cruces, New Mexico. I keep the date and place on a handwritten piece of paper that I have in my wallet, otherwise the that night would disappear from my memory forever.

The match was at a medium sized VFW hall, in a really shitty part of town. I was supposed to wrestle a luchador named El X. The guy had purposely fucked up one of my friend's knees about a year before. El X wasn't that big of a guy, he didn't even weigh 200 lbs., but the guy had a reputation for being an absolute psychopath. There were rumors that he shot up cocaine before each match. He was considered a 'person of interest' in the disappearance of a groupie after a match in Kingston, Arizona. He always went home to Mexico if any of his misdeeds caught up to him.

El X would always sell tickets to an event, which is why promotors continued to book him on both sides of the border. He was considered to be a bad guy, or a "heel" in wrestling vernacular, but fans would still cheer for him, they ate up his unpredictability. Most guys on the circuit wouldn't even get into the ring with him, even though it usually meant a pretty decent payday. You had to be in a rough way if you got into the ring with El X, or you had to be as fucking crazy as he was. I guess I was a little bit of both.

The two of us were the semi-main event, just before Terry Funk took on Abdullah the Butcher. We were scheduled to do a 20-minute match that would end a double disqualification. For the first ten minutes, I wondered if everything I heard about El X was wrong, he wrestled me cleanly and our styles seem to complement each other, I thought we were putting on a good show. At the eleven-minute mark, out of nowhere, for no reason, El X rammed his thumb into my eye socket. I just knew I was blinded. I was staggering, and could barely see when he picks me up and throws me over the top rope. My back hit the concrete, with nothing to break the fall. He jumps out of the ring and grabs a chair. I looked up to see it coming down on me, but not with the indented part, but sideways with the frame. I remember blood flooding into my uninjured eye, there was the sound of a bell, then just still darkness.

I had a patch over my left eye, and twenty-two stitches above right eye. My back was bruised, but there was no long-term damage that the doctors could find. Most of the promotors in the region liked me, but they wouldn't book me a match until I was healed. I was grateful for their concern, but I still had to make a living. There were bills to pay. An old tag team partner from my early days in the game drove down from Albuquerque to pick me up and let me stay with him while I recovered.

It was seven weeks before a promoter called. The guy who booked the Las Vegas shows said that there a was Battle Royal coming in a couple of weeks. It would be a low risk way to get back into the squared circle, and would let other promotors know that I was ready to work again. He said that if I came out early, he might be able to get me some autograph sessions to get me a few bucks. He even offered to let me stay in his pool house free of charge.

The guy told me to go to his gym, somebody named Freddy would help me get back in ring shape and tell me what plans for the match was, and what my role in the Battle Royal would be. When I got there, there were flyers to promote the night. My match was deep into undercard. I was the only one involved that had any kind of experience, for half the guys it would be there first time in a ring as a pro. The plan was that I would be the last to enter the ring, and I would be the third to the last out. There was a shudder of rage as I saw on the flyer that the main event was El X and some other luchador. I made up mind, right then and there that I was going to kill that mother fucker. I would just be one of fifty other guys in the dressing room that would be a suspect. At some point, at least a few of them had the same thought.

The night of the matches, there were whispers throughout the locker room wondering if El X would be able to perform that night. The rumor was that he had been on a two-day coke bender at a brothel outside of town. I overheard that he had beat up one of the girls pretty bad. I checked my bag to make sure that the hunting knife that I always carried was there.

The Battle Royal went off as planned, and my injuries didn't bother me at all. My vision was good, my back didn't bother me, and the stitches were replaced with a gnarly scar. Normally after I was done working, I would go to the bar or back to the hotel room. That night, I wanted to see the guy who jeopardized my career and livelihood.

Even as high and drunk as El X was, I gave him credit for still being able to do his job. He was a third-generation wrestler, it was in his blood, all he ever knew. Just like in my match with him, at first, he would be poetry to watch in the ring, a true technical professional. But in the end, something would snap inside of his brain, and he would become this sadistic demon. It happened that night, he bit a chunk out of the other guys forehead. When the night was over, most of the guys would have a little party. Usually backstage, everybody got along. My inner circle of people was all somehow involved in the business. My sex life was exclusive to groupies, marriage and wrestling didn't mix. Depending on what territory you were working in, it usually felt like family around you. The exception was El X, everybody hated him, including the other luchadores.

After his match, El X found a ratty couch in a corner of the dressing room and passed out, the days of partying had caught up to him. I made sure that I was one of the first to shower and leave the locker room. I told the other guys that I was going to skip the bar that night and go back to the hotel room. I wanted everybody to see me, I needed witnesses. I walked around the block a few times, to give the fans time to leave, then I went through a back door of the auditorium. From under the bleachers, I watched the locker room door. Nobody went in or out for fifteen minutes. I pushed through the door slowly, everybody else was gone, and El X was still on the couch.

I went and sat on a chair next to him. This was my chance, I could cut him up as he slept, but that's not how I wanted it to go down. I stripped naked, and went and turned one of the showers on. I jerked his shoulder until he stirred. I told him that he needed to shower and get out, the staff was trying to lock up. I told him I would help him. He groggily stood up and mumbled something incoherent as he walked to the shower. I held him steady as he pulled off his tights, then helped him into the water. As he rubbed his face in the water with his hands, I slammed my knife into him just above his belly button and sliced upward. He tried to scream, but no sound came out. I looked at him and asked if he remembered me. There was a look of horror on his face. I put the knife into his eye socket and twisted it.

The Las Vegas Police department spoke to every man who wrestled that night. They all told the same story, El X was passed out when they left, and they didn't see anything. There was no confrontation or argument they knew of. They told the cops, that everybody hated the dead man, and nobody was shedding tears over his demise. His opponent that night wasn't a suspect because he was in the hospital. The cops had nothing, no evidence, and the case eventually just went to the cold case file.

Word got around to the promotors that I was ready to get back in the ring with anybody. In my glory days, several years back, I signed a couple of contracts that kept me in an exclusive territory for whatever length of time. As my star power faded, I went independent to whoever offered me job. The fans still recognized my name, so I had enough of a reputation that I could always get booked. There was a family owned, start up promotion in Texas looking for has-beens like me to join them, they were offering contracts.

I ended up signing a six-month deal, and rented a studio apartment in San Antonio. The stars of the promotion were three young brothers, their father owned the outfit. In the ring, they portrayed the all-American Texas football boys, the t-shirts they sold had a picture of them on the front, and the words "God, Country, Family, and Wrestling" on the back. They were cheered wildly wherever they went. Around town, they were treated like rock stars.

That was their public persona, out of the spotlight they were three of the most self-destructive monsters you would ever want to meet. There were drugs everywhere, any wrestler in the promotion could get whatever they wanted. A few times the brothers would be taking turns with some girl backstage in front of everybody. It was routine for all them to get arrested, they wrecked cars, beat people up, and always had some type of narcotic on them. None of that ever made the news, they were legendary in the lone star state, the powers that be couldn't let the cash stop flowing.

The three brothers rarely wrestled outside of Texas, but the two younger brothers, the tag team champs, booked a month-long tour of Japan, and a few of us hopped into a rental van with the oldest brother, Kenny, the Mid-South heavyweight champion. Kenny could be very volatile. He had classic episodes of "roid rage". He always had a handgun to show off, but was never threatening with it. He could be an arrogant fuck too, but we were all was to each other.

One night in Topeka, Kansas, Kenny and I had adjoining rooms at a Holiday Inn. We closed the hotel bar down before going to our rooms. Kenny had been hitting on the waitress all night, a nice, pretty girl who I doubted was even old enough to be serving alcohol. She seemed annoyed at his advances, but somehow, he talked her into going to his room after she got off. I lay in my bed trying to get sleep, when I started hearing a banging sound from the room next door. Kenny was drunk and talking loudly, but I couldn't make out the words, something about "going to like it". The banging sound got louder, and I was sure that I heard crying. In about 15 minutes, I heard the door to Kenny's room slam. I peeked my head out the door to see the girl limping down the hall. There was blood running down her leg.

The next day, four of us drove to Colorado Springs. I was in the backseat behind Kenny wishing that I had a stretch of piano wire so that I could strangle him for what he had done to that girl, but I didn't let on that I knew anything. We didn't have to wrestle for a couple of nights, so we had some free time. Kenny wanted to head to the mountains to shoot guns. The other two guys said they just wanted to party. I told Kenny that I would go with him.

We passed a bottle of Jack Daniels back and forth as we drove, before stopping at a little canyon in the shadow of Pike's Peak. We used trees as targets as we walked through the forest drinking and shooting. I complimented Kenny on his gun, and he asked me if I wanted to try it. I took the 44 magnum and put it to his temple and pulled the trigger. I went back to the car, and drove to a cabin where I called 911. I told the operator that my friend had just shot himself. There sheriff questioned me about what had happened. I told him that Kenny was drunk, and distraught after he had confessed to raping somebody the night before. The girl reluctantly corroborated my story. The coroner declared Kenny's death a suicide, and that was the end of that. His dad even apologized to me for having to ne a witness to it, he said he always knew that would happen to Kenny.

It wasn't until 2006 that I killed anybody again, almost ten years after Kenny died. By that time, my wrestling career was pretty much over. I might do referee gigs occasionally if I missed being around the guys in the locker room. I had constant headaches, and couldn't stand the light. I worked the overnight shifts at a convenience store in Cheyenne, Wyoming because the brightness of daylight would debilitate me. I put aluminum foil in all of the windows in the trailer home I was renting to keep the light out. I lived by candlelight as much as I could.

If I wasn't working, I was drinking or sleeping. I often

had visions of the knife twisting in El X's eye, or Kenny's

brains dripping down a tree trunk. They were by no means

haunting visions, but more a source of comfort. With time, I

grew to think of those two occasions my proudest

accomplishments. I grew to think of myself as having done

those two pieces of shit a favor. I started to think of killing

people as philanthropy. I was going to make the world a

better place.

My third victim was a meth addict who lived in the drain culvert at the back of the trailer park. I told him that I had some really good dope, and he shot up a syringe full of bleach. As far as I knew, his death wasn't even investigated. In 2008, at a truck stop in Tulsa, I slit a guy's throat as he sat behind the wheel of his rig. I can't remember why I didn't like him. I killed two people in 2009, a girl in Boise who I picked up hitchhiking. It annoyed me that she didn't understand how dangerous it was for a pretty girl like her to be hitchhiking alone. I strangled her. A few days later I shot young man on a freeway in Spokane, but that was more of a road rage thing, so it doesn't really count.

I have vague memories of shooting a middle-aged couple as they slept in their tent at some campsite in a forest in Northern California. I don't remember the circumstances of those murders, but I think that happened in the summer of 2011. In January of 2013, I snuck into some lawyer's house in Phoenix and was going to stab him because I hated his fucking television commercials. I butchered him and it was messy. I wasn't expecting his wife to walk in on the grizzly sight, so I had to kill her too. I took a shower, stole some of the guy's clothes and left. At about midnight the same day, I was driving home from the bar when the flashing lights popped up in my rearview mirror.

I had surrendered myself to the thought that my time was up. They were going to give me the needle. I looked for my knife, but realized it was in the trunk. There was no point in resisting. I rolled down the window expecting the cop to have his gun drawn on me, instead he asked me how much I had to drink. I chose the path of least resistance and told the cop I was fucking hammered so he may as well just arrest me. The judge took note that I had four prior DUI's in Arizona alone, and more in other states. He sentenced me to two and half years. The bright lights in jail were excruciating to my brain. I would have episodes of paralysis. They let me serve most of my time in the infirmary. I have virtually no memory of my time in jail. My brain is funny. Some things I remember so vividly it's almost as if I am reliving the moment, other things I am told about and have no idea what they are talking about. There is no rhyme or reason as which is which.

After I got out of jail, I was declared disabled due to head trauma I had sustained during my career, so I didn't have to worry about work. I got a few bucks from class action concussion lawsuits against the wrestling industry. I moved to a little beach front bungalow in northern Oregon and did nothing but listen to ocean during the day, and watch it at night. Only occasionally would something remind me that I had killed several people over the course of my life.

In the fall of 2019, a ring booker that I had worked with in the 80's showed up at my door. He was working for a big national promotion that had several televised events per week. He told me that they were having a big reunion of former pro wrestlers in Las Vegas. They were going to use the event to create some kind of reality show. He made me a generous offer to be part of it, and I agreed but only after he assured me that the only time, I would have to leave my room is at night.

After dinner and a few speeches, we were encouraged by the producers to walk around, have cocktails and tell stories about old school wrestling. I was approached by a young guy, maybe 20, he was very handsome and had a familiar look about him. He explained that he was the son of one of the tag team partners I had in Georgia around 1990, we actually won the belts together. It made me feel good talking to the kid, I hadn't heard that his dad died of cancer last year. We laughed at stories he had heard as a kid about me and his dad on the road. I asked him what he was doing at the convention. He said that he was going to be on another one of the promotion's reality shows starring kids who were trying to embark on a life of pro wrestling.

I felt a surge of rage as he told me that. I've loved the wrestling game my entire life, but I wouldn't recommend it to my worst enemy, let alone some kid who has rose colored glasses on and expects the glory of professional wrestling that he sees on television. The cameras are rarely in the backstage area, and they are never in your hotel room. They don't capture the pain killers that it takes to get through the day. They don't tell you in wrestling schools that unless you are main event talent, you will probably only get paid enough to cover your hotel room, bar tab, and something to eat, leaving only enough for gas money to get to the next gig.

I invited the kid up to my room to smoke a joint. While he puffed, he asked me what it was like to be in a barbed-wire, steel cage match. I took off my shirt and showed him four-inch scar just below my right armpit. He told me how cool he thought it was. That made me smile, so I grabbed the hunting knife off of the night stand and jammed it into his Adam's apple. I just kept stabbing him. I tried to tell my brain to stop, but it wouldn't listen to me.

I sat down on the edge of the bed and looked around the room. Blood was everywhere, even on the ceiling. I had my doubts that I would get away with this one. I had the hotel's front desk call 911. One of the cops puked when he saw the scene in the room. In the interrogation room, I tried to explain that I went insane when the kid made a homosexual advance toward me. The detective laughed when I told him that.

I was formally charged with first degree murder. The district attorney told the judge he wanted more time to decide if he would be seeking the death penalty. I was acting as my own attorney; I made no objection to the request. Five weeks later, the DA told the judge he would not be seeking capital punishment but life without parole. I thought about those years I did in county on the DUI rap, and how bright it was in there. I remembered being on my bunk in a fetal position with my shirt over my head hoping the headache would stop.

I got a message to the DA, and told him I wanted discuss a plea deal. He came to the jail and told me that he didn't see any benefit to a plea, he had more than enough evidence to easily convict me.

"I'll tell you what," I said to him. "In exchange for you seeking the death penalty, I'll tell you about most of the murders I've been committing for thirty years. I can't tell you about all of them, because I don't remember them, I just know it happened"

He looked at me as though he thought I was trying to con him. "How many murders?"

"Probably 20-30"

"And you want to be sentenced to death? That's the opposite of how these negotiations go"

"Please don't be sarcastic. This is a genuine offer. We can both give what the other wants. I help you clean up a lot of cold cases, and you set me free......Not physically of course"

He sat down across the table and studied me. "The reason I didn't seek the death penalty for stabbing the young man is because I saw that you were on disability because of head trauma. The sentence never would have stood"

"My first murder was in June of 1995. A wrestler named El X. I butchered him in a shower in Las Vegas. That was years before I was diagnosed with a black brain. Several of them were"

"Why?" He shook his head in disbelief. "Why do you want to die?"

"One thing that my existence has taught is that nothing matters. Life is a façade. I see these people on tv chanting 'blue lives matter' or 'black lives matter' and the dumbest of all, 'all lives matter', and I just shake my head at their stupidity. So, when you ask me why I want to die, I just say its part of the process. Most people will never see it. On the grand scope of things, in my world, no lives matter, not even mine"

The Last Rag

I sat at the end of the pier hoping to watch the sunset, but the clouds weren't about to let that happen. The waves below were gentle, but when I looked back towards the shore there were still surfers trying to catch one. In that moment I felt their futility. They weren't going to ride any surf, and the wave that I had been riding the past two years was closing out. In a week and a half, my long dream would be coming to an end, life just like the decade. In just over four months, the 1980's would be upon us.

Ever since I was a kid, all I ever wanted to do was be a rock and roll writer. In those days, I had Christmas a few times a month. Every time an issue of Rolling Stone, Creem, or Circus came was like a holiday for me. I read every single word of each issue. In between issues of those rags, I filled my time with National Lampoon, Mad and for reasons other than writing, National Geographic. Every now and then, I would come across a copy of Playboy or Penthouse.

I idolized guys like Lester Bangs, Dave Marsh, P.J. O'Rourke and Hunter Thompson. There writing style was so fresh, unlike any of the crap that we were forced to read in school. Of course, I wanted to know about the bands I was listening too, but more than the story, I loved the way the aforementioned writers crafted their words. If two writers did the exact same interview with Iggy Pop, Lester Bang's piece would always be better.

Growing up, my dad was in the newspaper business. He was a stereotyper putting out the San Diego Union. He did a little photography work for the paper too. I loved going to see my dad at work. I loved the pace of the place, with an 11pm deadline, there was nobody just sitting around. Somebody was furiously doing something. The air was smoky, and cigarette butts swallowed up the cement floor. Seeing the presses spinning and smelling the ink was a wonderland for me. Like I said, there was nothing else that I ever wanted to be.

You couldn't write about rock and roll if you didn't know it, and I devoured it. All of it. My dad loved music, so it was always on at the house. "Rock Around the Clock" by Bill Haley and the Comets was a song I remember hearing while I was literally in the playpen. My dad liked the fifties stuff, like Elvis, Chuck Berry, Buddy Holly, and Jerry Lee Lewis to name a few. I had an older brother that listened to the sixties sound. You couldn't be from southern California and not like the Beach Boys, but he fully embraced the Rolling Stones and the Beatles during the British invasion. It was The Who that he probably listened to the most. I liked what mom listened to. She loved Frank Sinatra and Tony Bennett. Man, could she dance to Herb Alpert and the Tijuana Brass. She used to tease my dad that she was going to leave him for Bobby Vinton. Some of my friends would say that wasn't rock and roll, but it was to me.

From the time that I was nine, any time I would come across a few bucks, I would head to one of the records stores. I could spend all afternoon flipping through the vinyl, and often did. Anything I purchased, after I listened to it a few times, I would write a critique of it that nobody ever read. I did the same thing with songs that I heard on the radio. I used to write mock interviews with rock stars. I really liked one that I made up pretending to talk to Alice Cooper. They're probably still in a box somewhere in my mom's attic.

I sent stories to the big rock magazine but never got a response. I secretly knew that none of them was going to hire a 14-year-old surfer kid. I figured fuck them, I would start my own magazine. I was planning it right away. I dropped out of high school at 16 and got my GED. I took a job at a burger joint right on the beach. When my parents split up, and sold our house, I got a second job bussing tables at a night club that always featured live music. I was able to get a tiny studio apartment and still saved up enough money to print three small issues of the magazine.

I always knew what I would call the publication "The Ocean Beach Rock and Roll Rag". I put the first issue out when I was seventeen. It was a twelve-page tabloid. I had managed to sell a few small ads to defray the cost. The cover of the first issue was about a concert in the backyard of a house rented out by a bunch of surfers. Punk rock was really blowing up at the time, and the surfers persuaded a local band, The Raped, to play a party.

The leader of the band was a guy about my age who called himself Prick. The Raped had some notoriety around Ocean Beach. The had recorded a four song EP and pressed 500 vinyl copies. They sold out in less than a week and partied the money away. The band was going to have play some gigs before they could afford to press any more. In that first issue I wrote about how good they were live, even if it was on a small brick patio in a backyard. I gave them a great rating for their self-titled EP. The only thing that would have made it better was an interview with Prick himself.

That would never happen, because the reputation was

Prick didn't speak to anyone. The only time words came out

of his mouth was when he was singing, if that's what you

want to call it. For being so small in stature, he had a look of

wild-eyed rage about him. He was not somebody to be

fucked with. I tried to explain who I was at the party, but he

just glared at me as he walked by. They had two more shows

after the back yard, and I went to both of them. Prick was too

fucked up for me to even attempt an interview. Both places

were packed. There were people driving down from LA to

see them. After a show at Winston's on the Beach, The Raped

just vanished. Nobody had heard from any of the members. I

was disappointed that I never got to talk to prick.

People seemed to take to The Ocean Beach Rock and Roll Rag. By the time the fourth issue came out, I had two other writers helping me, and was selling enough advertising to keep us solvent. By our twelfth issue, there were six writers and a saleswoman. We had reached a point that were actually getting weekly paychecks, none of them ever reaching three figures. Here I was, just shy of 19, and I was living my life's dream.

Record companies started sending us free promotional records to review. They would also send us concert tickets if the venue didn't invite us themselves. I got backstage passes for the Rolling Stones in Anaheim on the 1978 tour. Ron Wood shook my hand, and gave me a cheesy quote for a story. I got to hang with Van Halen after they warmed up Black Sabbath at the Sports Arena in late 1978. They were a great group of guys, and I knew they were going to be huge.

By the spring of 1979 I began to realize that my dream was slowly crumbling. Everybody that was working on the magazine was partying too hard to continue the success. By the time June came around every single staffer had mirror with cocaine on their desk. It was a nonstop party 24 hours a day. Deadlines were getting missed and the quality of writing slid with each issue. We were barely talking to each other. You can't run a magazine without communicating. We started to live the life of rock stars instead of chronicling it.

The unsurvivable wipeout came on the Fourth of July of that year. A veteran writer, 20 years old than the rest of us, who we had hired just two months earlier, was arrested for having sex with a 14-year-old boy in the back of his car behind a punk venue downtown. It turned into a big story, the news outlets kept referring to him as a "reporter for the Ocean Beach Rock and Roll Rag". By the end of the week, every single advertiser we had cancelled their business. The rest of the staff saw the writing on the wall and scattered like cockroaches. I wasn't ready for it to end. I had enough money that I decided I was going to put out one last issue, and I was going to do it the same way I did the first issue, by myself.

With no advertising, I had the freedom to do whatever the fuck I wanted with those pages. Column inches would only be a marginal worry. I didn't have to worry about some customer being offended by some petty insignificance. I was in no hurry. I could use about two-thirds of the magazine reprinting the best articles of the past two years. I would spend some space on "goodbye" interviews with people in the music business with whom I had become friends with over the past two years. I thought there should be a larger story trying to offer some kind of explanation about the incident involving the writer and 14-year-old boy. The only thing I didn't have was a cover story.

That's why I was on the pier feeling sorry for myself, looking for some inspiration. The cloud bank on the horizon was the perfect symbol for how I was feeling about the cover. I walked back down the pier and sauntered around the beach, walking through the foamy water. There were ideas racing around my brain, but none of them were the bang that I wanted to go out with for the final edition of "The Rag".

I found my way back to the office, above a head shop on Newport Avenue. I smoked a joint hoping for some spark of creativity. There were no really big shows coming up, and the acts that were in town didn't deserve much coverage even if it wasn't the last issue. I looked around the room wondering how the hell I was going move everything out. I might just leave it for the landlord to throw it into the alley after he does the eviction. I would have to sleep on the cover for another night.

As I was turning off the light and walking out the door, something caught my eye. Hanging on the wall just left of the door, was a framed copy of the very first edition of The Ocean Beach Rock and Roll Rag. There was a picture of The Raped playing in those surfers' backyard. It was perfect. I would send the magazine out the way it came in. I was going to track down the members of the band. I decided right then and there, if he was still alive, I was going to interview Prick.

The bass player was easy to find. He filled in for several bands around the San Diego when they needed some bass. I caught up with him subbing for a ska band in Orange County. He was a good musician, but too monotone to make for a good interview. He told me that the drummer had quit music and was working at a casino in Primm, Nevada. The guitarist had drowned in a surfing accident. When I asked him about Prick, he just shrugged his shoulders and shook his head. The bassist said the last he heard Prick was somewhere in Hollywood, but he guessed he had od'd by then.

I asked everybody on the scene if they heard from Prick. The stories were all over the board. He was in L.A. He was in New York. He was in jail. He was dead. He met a girl and had a baby. He was doing gay porn. Nobody was sure about anything they said. Still, I had enough gut feelings to know he wasn't in San Diego and the best educated guess was somewhere in LA.

I knew my way around the Hollywood music venues and had made some friends while running the magazine. Despite the geographical distance, almost everybody knew who Prick and The Raped were. The EP that they released had a cult following. It was getting passed around on cassette tapes. One guy told me there were a lot of people looking for Prick, mostly sleazy music business assholes. He told me to go talk to the doorman of the punk club down the street. Finally, I got a solid lead. The doorman told me that Prick was in San Francisco living with a girl. He said that Prick was using a lot of heroin, but as far as he knew, he was still alive. He gave me the name of a sex club that he heard the girl worked at and described her to me.

It was ten at night when the doorman gave me that information. There was still a little bit of money in the magazines checking account, but I decided to be thrifty and drive through the night to the bay area. I pulled over a couple of times to nap, and I filled my gut with a stale bag of potato chips that had been in the car for quite some time. By the time I saw the city, it occurred to me that I didn't know the first thing about San Francisco.

After getting lost several times, the girl ended up being exactly where the doorman in Hollywood said she would be. It was a sign, a minor miracle. She was the most vacant person I have ever met. It went beyond the drugs, she was flesh and blood, and moved, but it was like there was no soul inside her. I looked around the sex club, concluding having no soul might actually be an asset in the place. When I told her who I was, and who I was looking for, she seemed suspicious. To save us both time I gave her $10 and she told me where Prick was.

I found him in an old custodial room of a semi-abandoned warehouse. I say "semi-abandoned" because there were enough homeless people in there to make a small town. Pricks face was still the same, kinda, at least enough for me to recognize him, or I wouldn't have believed it was him. When he played the show in the backyard, he had that tan athletic surfer body, now he was just grey skin stretched out over his skeletal system. His hair was long and matted. His eyes were closed but I could see that he was breathing. I called him by name, but that didn't rouse him. I wasn't about to fuck with his high, so I just sat down and waited. I was tired from driving all night.

I guess I dozed off and when I woke up Prick was still high, but I could tell it was wearing off. I don't know how long I sat in the corner before I realized he was lucid and looking at me, but he didn't say anything. The funny thing is, his eyes were fiery, it wasn't something I would have expected from a junkie. I asked him what his name was, but he didn't answer. When I asked if his name was Prick, his eyebrows raised sharply, but he still didn't say anything. I told him the story about seeing The Raped play in the backyard of a surfer house and now I was running a rock and roll magazine in San Diego –

"San Diego?" those were the first words I ever heard him say other than when he was singing.

"Yeah"

"Are you from San Diego?"

"Yes"

His voice got melancholy, "Fuck I miss San Diego"

"So, do I, I have been gone trying to track you down for almost two weeks."

"Track me down?"

I told him the whole sordid story of the magazine, how The Raped was on the cover of the first issue and about all of the shows that I went to and the parties and how it all went to our heads and that we partied a really good magazine away and now I was broke and was going to put out one last issue and that I wanted to interview him for it.

"Are you driving a car?"

"Yeah"

"And you want to interview me?"

"It would be a great way to send the magazine out"

"If you give me ride home to San Diego, you can ask me whatever you want"

"We can do that"

"Is it a paid interview?

"I guess I can give a few bucks"

"$40?"

I looked in my wallet, "All I have is $37 on me"

"Good enough. I need to pick up some supplies for the drive"

Prick fixed up just before he got in the car heading south. I figured that he would be out for a while. I really wanted to interview him and I figured there might be only so much time where he was coherent enough to talk. If I took the interstate, I may be robbed of some of those moments. There was no good reason not to take Highway One down the coastline. I had nowhere to be and I was sure his only concern was running out of heroin.

I was listening to The Clash's "London Calling" north of San Luis Obispo when I noticed that Prick had his eyes open. He was awake. He was more than awake, he was alert. He must have been having some type of sensory overload. He was shaking.

"Stop the car"

"There's a pullout just ahead"

When I parked the car, he got out and slowly walked over to the edge of a cliff above the crashing water. He moved his head back and forth, just spanning the horizon up and down. I could tell that he was trying to control his breathing. He sat down in the dirt with his legs crossed and face in his hands sobbing. I grabbed the camera out of the car and started taking his picture.

When we were back on the road, Prick's demeanor was completely different. He actually started making small talk. I had to remind him again of who I was and what I wanted. After that, he just started talking freely, I didn't really have to ask him any questions, he just started talking. I put my mini tape recorder on the dash. He started telling me what he had been doing lately. He said that he was trying to get a band together, but some guys in San Francisco ripped off all of his equipment. He tried to make his life sound like he wasn't a total junkie, but he knew he wasn't fooling me and just gave up. "What else do want to know about me?"

"The girl," I said. "Where did you meet up with her?"

"What girl?"

"Your girlfriend that you met in LA"

"What the fuck are you talking about?"

"The girl, whatshername, she works at the sex club. She told me where to find you"

The was a look of sincere confusion on Prick's face. I think he was trying to decide whether he should be sad or angry. The anguish on his face showed it all. "I need a fix" He was out of it the rest of the day. One of the few friends that I have who is not in the music business lived in Long Beach. He said we could crash there for the night; he was going out and we could make ourselves at home. We both went right to sleep.

It was close to noon, on southbound I-5 when he started talking as freely as he did the day before. We were driving through Carlsbad and he pointed out places where he had surfed and even described the waves he rode. These kind of surfing stories went on all the way down the coast until we got to Ocean Beach.

"Why don't you sleep at the newspaper office tonight. I only want to talk to you about music. We've hardly talked about it since we left San Francisco. There are beds there, nobody will bother us. Unless you have somewhere else to go"

"I gotta shoot first"

While Prick got high, I went home and got cleaned up. It seemed like I had been gone for too long. I went over and said hello to a couple of friends, picked up some high-quality coke, then went to another friend's that had just got back from Tijuana with some good tequila. When I got back to the office, he was still comatose. My stomach grumbled and it took me a while to remember when the last time I ate was. I went down the street to order a pizza to go and had a couple of beers with the owner while it cooked. We had become friends because he also owns a music club down by the beach. I took the pie back to the office hoping Prick would be lucid, but he wasn't. I had a few lines and a couple of shots by the time I heard him say, "can I have a piece of that pizza?"

"Help yourself"

As he ate his slice, he looked around the room at all the music shit hanging on the wall. He got up to take a closer look at all of it. He kept laughing to himself without saying what he was looking at. Some of the articles he appeared to read all of the way through. Eventually, he got to the framed first edition by the door. He seemed a little taken aback at first, then moved in for a closer look. "Do you have one of these that I can read, that isn't in a frame?" I went and got one from the cabinet and handed it to him. He read every word of it.

"That seems so far away"

"When you told me that you were trying to put a band together in San Francisco, was that true?"

"Fuck no. That was junkie talk. I haven't even sung with the radio since I left Ocean Beach"

"Do you still follow the scene?"

"I hear things, but not really"

I snorted a line, got up and walked around the desk so I could study his face, "you have no idea that you are a cult hero, do you?"

He half laughed, "a cult hero?" I could tell by the look on his face that he had no idea what I was talking about.

I'm not sure if junkies are able to muster a look of stunned surprise, but that was the only way I could describe Prick's face as I told him that the EP that The Raped had recorded was an underground cult classic, that people had photocopies of the cover in frames on their walls and that since nobody could buy the EP, it got passed around on shitty quality cassette tapes. He didn't know that there were record companies looking to buy the rights.

"If word got out that you were here," I told him. "Within an hour there would be line of people at the door waiting to get your autograph. If they heard that you were going to be on a stage tonight, the place would sell out to the rafters. You're a fucking legend in OB"

He looked scared, he might have even been having a panic attack. "Can I use your phone?" He called somebody for a ride. He said there was no way he could live in OB if that's how people were going to treat him. He had a brother living in Imperial Beach. He would lay low there for a while.

"Thanks for the ride. And the pizza" he said as he walked out the door. I immediately sat down at the typewriter.

I once again had no way to get ahold of Prick if I had any follow up questions. I put the issue out anyway. I wasn't sure how it would go over with the scandal still going through courts. There were a couple of people who accused me of making the story up because Prick had died a year ago. The record companies were calling the office constantly, begging for information on where they could find him. The issue disappeared as fast as it went out, but was so well talked about that the guy that owned the record store offered to pay to print more. He was so happy that the next printing disappeared as fast as the first, we decided to form a partnership where he would finance the next six copies, provided that I did it all myself, and only put it out once a month. He would take care of all the financial and business aspects of "The New Ocean Beach Rock and Roll Rag"

The day the second edition of the new format came out, I had to start thinking about the third. It was hard work putting out a magazine by yourself. It was a seven day a week, minimum 12-hour day, and I loved every minute of it. Every now and then somebody from one of the big magazines would come down from LA and take me to lunch and ask me if I was happy doing it, because they said they could always use another good writer on the staff, and that the perks were unbelievable. I would thank them for lunch, and tell them that I had an agreement with the record store owner to put out six issues.

While I was listening to some vinyl that a record company and planning the third issue in December of 1979, there was a knock at the door. I yelled at whoever it was to come in. I looked at the figure and turned the music down. I would have loved to seen the look on my face. "Holy Fuck Prick, what happened to you?"

"My brother got me on a program. Got me clean.
Haven't had heroin in 43 days"

"You look good," he did to, he had put on some
weight, he had a tan, and he was smiling. I had never seen
that before. He was surfing again.

"Are you looking for a story?"

"Always"

"I'm giving this to you exclusively, you can break it. I
sold the rights to the EP. It's going be out in the spring of next
year"

"That's fucking nuts bro, congratulations"

"My brother is smart. He stayed in school, went to
college, he set it all up"

"Are you going to record more? Do some shows?"

"Nah, I'm not even sure that's what I wanted when I
was 16, and I know for fucking sure that I don't want it at 20.
I might stay in the music business though"

"Oh yeah, what are you going to do?"

"I'm going to go to Nashville, change my name and just see what happens." As he walked out the door, he said he would stay in touch.

After the sixth issue, the record store owner and I amicably went our separate ways, and "The New Ocean Beach Rock and Roll Rag" was no more. I spent the next couple of years freelancing for big publications still writing about rock and roll but that wore thin real fast because music in the eighties was so fucking shitty. I sold a couple of screenplays and continue to write them to this day.

Prick ended up in Memphis instead of Nashville, and he tried to get some bands together, but it never happened. He carved out a little niche doing some songwriting, including a couple of decent hits for country stars. Seven years after leaving Ocean Beach clean and sober, his demons finally tracked him down. He od'd under a bridge near the Mississippi River.

Shumana

There were sirens and flashing lights in my neighborhood so often, I barely noticed them anymore. In the middle of the night, depending the situation, the first responders are usually very courteous and turn the sirens off when they pulled in from the main road. So, I knew something pretty bad was happening when an extended barrage of emergency vehicles skidded into the townhouse complex at 1:36 on a Sunday morning. I got out of bed and went to the patio. One of the homes on the next street over had flames shooting out of its roof. I stood outside in the night and watched until the fire was put out about an hour later.

I tried to go back to bed, but I was a little too wired from the excitement. Tried to watch tv, but nothing hooked me. I went to the refrigerator to look for a snack, but sat down at my desk with a beer instead. I got online, searched for any news about the fire, but there was nothing this soon after it happened. I knew all of the baseball scores, but checked to see if I had missed any. I can't be at my laptop, and at least see if there is anything that looks interesting on Pornhub. I like the ones where a muscular black dude with a huge dick fucks a young skinny white chick.

I had been trying to avoid Facebook, too many fucking idiots. I don't even know how I know my friends. I was running out of my usual sites, but I knew I would just stare at the ceiling if I went back to bed. I logged on and looked at the notifications that had been waiting for me. The one at the top of the list said "Shumana 'is' live". I usually see these after the fact. Most of her live sessions are from some random billiards bar where she was hustling a few bucks. I rarely went back and watched them. At that hour, I doubted that she could be shooting pool, so I was curious about what she was doing, and to be honest, I really didn't have anything else to do.

Her live feed may as well have been a still frame, her phone propped up against something and capturing a shot of a white living room in complete disarray. There were turned over bar stools in the middle of the room. In the background, it might have been a fish tank that has been smashed. One wall had the holes in it, like somebody had punched it. There was the sound of soft crying that would intermittently turn into loud sobs. "I could die right now" a shaking voice said. I couldn't be sure if that was Shumana speaking or not. "I'm going to die right now"

I looked at the comment section, they were coming in faster than I can read them. From what I gathered, it seemed Shumana and some guy had been drinking for about two days straight and that a physical fight had started before Shumana had turned on Facebook live. There were several comments popping up that the police had been called and they would be there shortly. The broadcast had been going for 39:41 minutes when a huge crash happened off camera. A series of loud screams could be heard, followed by a rapid sequence of gunshots. Then there was about a minute of total silence. You could hear somebody knocking at a door. There was one more gun shot. There was a loud noise, and from the left side of the screen a figure runs into the middle of the room. It is a cop with his gun drawn. He surveys the room and turns to shout "We need two ambulances right fucking now." He sees the phone. The screen goes dark.

I met Shumana on February 17, 2008. It's easy for me to remember that date because I had spent the past five days in Las Vegas. I had been married by Elvis on Valentine's Day at a little chapel on the strip just the Friday prior. I had spent the weekend telling my new wife, Sunny, what a good husband I was going to be to her. We barely left our hot tub suite at the MGM until our flight out Sunday afternoon.

The boss told me before I left for vacation that she had hired a new girl that would be sitting in the cubicle across from me. I was a little bummed out that I was going to have to share my far back dark corner of the second floor. When I got in that Monday morning, and sat at my cubicle I looked over at my new colleague, but her back was to me so that all I could see was long, shiny jet-black hair that stretched to her lower back.

My boss, a lovely woman, peeked her head around the corner of the cube, "Miles," she said, "do you have a sec?"

"Sure"

She went over and tapped the new girl on the shoulder, "Shumana?"

The girl looked up, "yes?"

The boss pointed at me, "Shumana, this is Miles, Miles this is Shumana."

We both smiled and said "nice to meet you" at the same time.

There was some small talk between the three of us, but I don't remember because, holy fuck! Shumana was hot, stunningly beautiful. Her face was as flawless as her hair, big brown eyes, perfect white teeth and a smooth dark complexion. Her body was incredible, she was taller, and she was on the lean-to muscular side. She had to be some type of athlete. Here I was, on my third full day of being a husband for the second time, and I could feel myself getting a hard on for Shumana.

She turned out to be very friendly and we hit it off right away. We started going to lunch together a couple of times a week. She seemed really fascinated with the fact that I was newly married. She asked me if anything had changed? Had the sex had got better or worse? I was honest with her in an explicit way and started describing to her in detail how good the sex was with my wife. Shumana was married too, and had been that way for six years. She was nonchalant in talking about her sex life. She was bi, like my wife, and her husband liked to her watch her with other girls. They would go to the strip club and find a dancer to bring home. She confessed that she liked to see her husband's dick in a stripper, but wished he would put it in her more. Her behavior towards me got more risqué by the day.

It was three months to the day of meeting Shumana, a warmer than usual spring day in May, she was wearing a tight stretching, black sleeveless dress, its hem only coming to mid-thigh. She was unusually quiet that day, but we had both been given big projects and maybe she was just busy. At about three that afternoon, she turned and faced her chair towards me. She used her index finger to motion me closer. I wheeled my chair into her cubicle and she asked me what my wife and I were going to do that night. I told her that my wife was bartending, so she wouldn't be home until early in the morning. I wondered why she asked. She whispered that she had told her husband about me and he suggested that the four of us get together and that if things went well, we could all end up naked on the same bed. I told her that I thought I could get Sunny to warm to the idea.

We heard the boss on the next row over, so I slid my chair back into by cubicle but I was looking at her the entire time. I could feel my erection and knew it was visible through my dress slacks. She pulled the hem of her dress up to her hips, and spread her legs. With two fingers, she started playing fingering her bald pussy. The sound of the boss calling for a quick meeting put an abrupt halt to my little show.

In corporate America, there is no such thing as a quick meeting, this one went until 15 minutes after the office was supposed to close. Everybody else on the floor scurried to get the hell out of the building, all of them cussing under their breath. I was going to do the same until Shumana grabbed my arm. We stay motionless until we heard the door close for the last time and the floor was silent. She guided me to sit down, then pulled her dress up to her waist and straddled me. She grinded her wet spot into my zipper. We kissed a couple of times before she slid off my lap to her knees on the floor. I undid my belt, and unzipped my pants. She sucked hard and deep and swallowed all of it.

We promised that we wouldn't do anything again until our spouses were with us. Sunny was willing to see what happened, and her husband was cool, all that was left to do was figure out when we are all free. Shumana set it all up on Wednesday, we were going to go to a motel that had a clothing optional pool. She thought that would be a great way for all of us to get to know each better. There were two rooms booked for Saturday night. We spent all day Thursday telling each other how excited we were and make up dirty fantasies about what might happen.

On Friday morning, Shumana still wasn't at her desk by ten. I tried to call and text her, but there was no response. I asked the boss if she knew what was up, she told me that she wasn't supposed to say anything, but Shumana's husband had been in a pretty serious motorcycle accident the night before. All she knew was that he was in intensive care.

Shumana ended up taking a leave of absence from work to take care of her husband. It was a couple of weeks before she texted me and told me that her husband was home from the hospital, but that he was in a lot of pain. He had broken his left leg in four places, fractured his pelvis, and there were some cracked vertebrae in his lower back, but he wasn't paralyzed. They had sent him home with a lot of pain medication. She said she was really liking his Oxycontin. She profusely apologized that we were not able make the little rendezvous with our spouses happen. She said that she was really looking forward to it.

Three weeks after she came back to work, Shumana was one of the ones caught up in a mass round of layoffs. When she came to say goodbye to me, she was very upset, makeup was running down her cheeks from the tears. She was distraught over how she was going to survive since her husband couldn't work and his attorney had yet to work out a settlement with the insurance company. I hugged her and told her to relax. The company was generous with their severance packages, and she could get unemployment. We agreed to have lunch the next week.

We ended up nixing the lunch idea, and went to happy hour instead. Shumana was still beautiful, but she wasn't radiating it, she looked tired and just a little out of it.

"How's your husband?"

She shrugged her shoulders and pursed her lips, "I don't know. He's not getting any better, and it doesn't seem like he's even trying"

"How about you? How are you doing?"

"I'm bored out of my mind. Before the wreck, we were hardly ever at home, now we barely leave the house"

"Can he still fuck you?

She looked at me coyly, "let's do a couple of shots," she called the bartender over and ordered a couple of Jack Fire shots. I just listened as she talked about her life. Much of it made no sense, but I humored her and she smiled. We did two more shots.

She put her hand on my thigh, and whispered into my ear, "No, Miles, he can't fuck me. He won't be able to for at least a couple more months"

"Oh shit, Shumana, that's gotta suck for you"

"Not really, he has figured it out that he likes to watch me with other guys more than he likes to watch me with other girls"

"Oh yeah….?" I've always loved when women tell me their dirty stories.

"One night I was in tears because I was so horny, and couldn't get him hard. He was embarrassed and felt so bad, he told me that I should go to the bar, pick up a guy and bring him home. I tried to talk him out of it, but he said he understood that I had needs"

"That's pretty cool of him, I'd do the same thing, in fact it turns me on to watch"

"I picked out this young guy, I had heard him say his 21st birthday was a week ago. I started flirting with him and challenged him to a game of pool. He got cocky and talked shit. He accepted a little wager; mother fucker had no idea I competed national tournaments. The wager was that whoever lost had to do anything the winner asked. He got even cockier, which was cute, because he was such an innocent boy. I let him break, then I cleared the table. You should have seen the look on his face when I told him that since he lost, he had to come to my house and fuck me in front of my husband"

I almost spit out my beer I laughed so hard, "Oh man, I would have loved to have seen that look"

"It was hilarious. But it turned out to be shitty, he was a kid and I was too much for him. He came in about two minutes and was too nervous to get it up again. I think my husband was more disappointed than I was. He said I could try again the next night if I wanted to"

I was still laughing at her story, "how did you make that poor boy cum so fast?"

"I was just giving him head and I didn't even get fucked. So, anyway, the next night I purposely dressed a little slutty, and went to this bar I used to go to when I was single. As soon as I got there, this older black guy started hitting on me. He was in his fifties, but he must have been a football player or a bodybuilder, he was big and muscular…."

I interrupted her, "I've told my wife I had fantasies about watching her with a black guy, so if you tell me what I think you're about to tell me, I'm going to get very turned on"

Shumana smiled, put her hand on my dick, and leaned into me, "the dude said he would have no problem fucking me in front of my husband. He had done it before, and liked it. This guy spent what seemed like an eternity just licking and fingering my pussy, I was delirious at how good it felt. My husband was rubbing himself. My lover stood up, there wasn't an ounce of fat on his body, and his dick, fucking huge, I could put both hands on it and still have some in my mouth. I thought I was going to pass out when he put it in my pussy. I have had some good fucks in my life, but nothing like that mother fucker"

I told Shumana how hard my dick was just from listening to her, and told her that I would love to have sex with her while her husband watched. "Funny you should mention that," she said. "We were just talking about that, even though he can't play, he said I should invite you and Sunny over and the three of us could naked and nasty"

We set it up for two nights later. Sunny was turned on by the thought so much we had sex on the dining room table right after I told her. The next morning, my phone had 18 missed calls from Shumana. I tried repeatedly to call her back, but there was no answer. I noticed that there was a voice mail alert. Her husband was dead. He od'd. She would call me later.

Sunny and I went to the funeral but really didn't get to talk to Shumana. Soon thereafter, her phone was disconnected. I didn't have any contact with her in more than a year until I received a Facebook request from her. We messaged each other inconsequential shit every now and then, but it was obvious that Shumana didn't want to be bothered at this point in her life.

It had probably been at least six months since our last communication, but Shumana reached out to me after I posted on Facebook about the passing of my wife. She was just doing her usual Sunday afternoon bartending shift when a brain hemorrhage hit. She died in the ambulance on the way to the hospital. Shumana wanted to come over and cook me dinner, and just talk because she had relatable experience. I knew she did, and she was just trying to be nice, but I was inconsolable at that time. I stayed in my empty home alone for months, getting drunk and passing out, then waking up and doing it again and again. Just when I thought I was on the verge of ending up in a mental institution, I opted to go be a hermit at a small cabin in Oregon for fourteen months.

When I returned from my self-imposed exile, I posted it on Facebook to see if any of my old friends wanted to get together for a drink, a few of them responded, but I was surprised that Shumana was one of the first. The next night, I picked her up at her townhome where she was living with her mother and drove to some overpriced wing joint that she used to work at. In the few years since I had last seen her, she looked different. She was still beautiful, but she had lost a lot of weight that she didn't have to lose. She looked gaunt.

She was more subdued and sullener than I had ever seen her before. Normally, she was on the boisterous side and constantly laughing, but that night there was a sadness about her. We sipped our drinks and talked about our departed spouses. She told me that she took her mom in after the police found her sleeping in alley with a .364 blood alcohol content.

"She's pretty much been drunk her entire life, ever since she left the reservation"

"I guess I never knew you were native American"

"Half Hopi Indian, half white. I never met my father, and my mother only met him the onetime"

"Is 'Shumana' a Hopi name?"

"Yeah, it means rattle snake girl"

"I can see that"

"Damn right, some mother fucker messes with this he gets a poisonous bite"

I teased her that I would like to suck the venom out of her, she got a seductive look, but pushed me back when I tried to kiss her. She said she had to the bathroom. She had barely closed the door when she stormed back to the table, she was in panic, said she needed get home right away.

"Is everything okay?" I asked as I was driving.

She took a deep breath, "it's okay. I just had a panic attack"

"Is it okay? What were you panicking about?"

She gave me a sad look, but there was brief silence before she spoke, "Sorry dude, I just freaked out when I found out that I left my cocaine at home"

"Damn girl, you must be hitting that shit hard"

"At least a teener a day. Every day, for the last three and a half years"

"Holy shit! That's gotta get expensive"

"I have a few bruthas that no how to hook a girl up"

When I dropped her off, she ran to the door. She needed that blow bad. I was assuming that would be the last time I ever saw Shumana.

We would chat a little bit every few months but I always knew what she was up to, because she turned her Facebook page into her personal YouTube channel. She was constantly going live. The usual "look at me" shit, and if she wasn't live, she was posting selfies. She checked in everywhere she went. When she went to New Mexico or Arizona, she checked in every hundred miles. Over the past year, she started wearing a tiara everywhere she went. I thought it was a joke at first, but then she changed her screen name to "Queen Shumana". She started wearing just outlandish makeup. I wanted to reach out to her to see if I could help her, but by then we were no longer chatting.

It didn't take a shrink to know that Shumana was having a bi-polar meltdown and broadcasting it to everyone. Her life was one crisis after another and was always asking for money. I lost count of how many times her car got towed. It seemed like she was in the hospital every other month. I unfollowed her a couple of times because it was too depressing to watch, but curiosity always got the best of me.

It was only two months ago, she started posting about being excited about going on a cruise to somewhere out of Miami. She started doing live broadcasts as soon as she got to the airport. It was all for naught. The guy that she thought she was meeting there, never showed. He had promised to pay for everything, she was stuck in South Beach without a dollar to her name. There was a live feed of Shumana crying, and begging any of her friends to send her money so she could get a hotel room. Two nights later, she went live while she was making out with a girl in a room full of Cuban guys. A few days later she posted that she was home and that she was going to be getting off of Facebook for a while.

Shumana started getting on social media again. She was just asking for prayers for her mother who was apparently in a coma in the intensive care unit. I was a bit jaded by then, so I didn't comment until I knew this wasn't just another scam for money, I followed her page until I was convinced her mother really was sick, so I messaged her to let me know if she needed anything.

When her mother passed a few days later, I texted her again to ask if there was anything I could do. She replied that she wanted me to take her golfing. It wasn't the answer I was expecting, but it was Shumana I was dealing with after all. She met me in the parking lot of the golf course. When she got out her car, she looked horrible. Her skin had a yellowish hue to it, and bruises covered her arms and legs. It was obvious she was trying cover up the scabs on her face with makeup. There was frailty in her walk. Beads of sweat were forming at the base of her tiara. I asked how she was, and she mumbled something incoherent. I suggested that maybe we should reschedule for when she was feeling better. She nodded in agreement and said thank you.

That was the last time I heard her voice until I heard her say "I'm going to die right now" on her video. Though the image was gone, dozens of her friends were still commenting on what was going on. Somebody had gone to her house, and was commenting from the scene. He said that paramedics had just gone. He said there wasn't much activity going on in the house, and he didn't think that was a good sign. Then he wrote that the paramedics were leaving the house with their gurneys empty. A lot of unmarked cop cars were pulling up. He wrote, "RIP Shumana"

The Tent in the Park

I'd owned my home for 22 years, and have only lived in five different houses in my life. I have not have had enough of a background to make the assumption that probably every neighborhood in America has a guy like my next-door neighbor, Luther. The guy that appoints himself the sheriff of the street. He's the one that will call the homeowner's association the day after somebody's car license plate expires. He takes walks around the neighborhood at both dawn and dusk, wearing camouflage pants and holding a mini-notebook. There is an oversized Ford dually pick-up parked out his front with a big American flag in the bed. He always has one earphone in so he can listen to the police scanner.

Luther moved in three years after I did. He had a wife who was rarely seen outside, and two daughters that I had watch grow up. We live in an upscale neighborhood right at the foothills in Littleton. I am an attorney; I own the Michael Spinuzzi Law Firm. Luther owns some kind heating and plumbing business. I've never been too tight with him, but we are pleasant to each other. We used to know each other better before my divorce. My wife used to adore his two daughters.

There was a lot of drama in the neighborhood, sometimes it felt like I was living in the middle of one of those prime-time soap operas that were popular in the 80's. There was always some type of tension on the cul-de-sac. The street, and the front of my house were to be avoided at any cost. I parked in the garage, used the back door and if I was going outside, it was to my backyard on the hill over the park. I worked a lot too, so my involvement with my neighbors was minimal. A Jeffco Sherriff car was on our street at least a couple of times a week, but it never involved me.

If I did run into somebody from the street, I would try to be polite as they caught me up on the neighborhood gossip. There are eight houses on the street, and I am Switzerland, the neutral one, so that leaves seven, and six of those are occupied by somebody with a serious addiction issue, be it alcohol or pills. They had issues among themselves, but they were all in agreement that they hated the neighbor in the seventh house, and Luther hated them all back. He had told me once that he had served in the first Iraq war, and I sometimes wondered if he thought of all of humanity as his enemy.

There was a gate in my fence that opened to a path leading down to the park, and I would occasionally go walk around the pond. Once the Coronavirus Lockdown hit, and we weren't supposed to leave our houses, I walked around the park multiple times per day. In the evenings, I started noticing a teenage boy, probably 16 or 17, with long brown hair who would lay his head on his big backpack in a grove of trees. One morning just before sunset, he was sleeping on one of the wrought iron memorial benches. He started sitting at a picnic table all day. As far as I knew, he never bothered anybody.

On the day of the summer solstice, I headed down the path for a late afternoon walk. There was an odd sound, a squeak mixed with a grinding noise. It became ear piercing the closer I got. As I rounded a bed of sunflowers and looked over the playground where a girl was on unoiled swing set. She was pulling back on the chains violently and kicking her feet hard, she was trying to get as high as she could, like she was about to launch herself somewhere. Like the boy, this twelve-year-old girl with blue hair was becoming a near constant presence in the park.

A couple of the neighbors had flagged me down, to say that there was going to be a block party on the Fourth of July complete with fireworks from Wyoming. The lady across the street from me was going to put tables in her garage for pot luck dinners. I told her I would join in an order some pizza. I just had to supply my own booze, but I bought a keg so that everybody could have some.

At nine o'clock, two of the guys started shooting off the fireworks, and they were as annoying as I had always found them to be, but I was buzzed and a lady who I didn't recognize was hitting on me, so I ignored them. Fifteen minutes later Luther went over to the men lighting the fuses and loudly told them that fireworks were prohibited by the HOA as well as county ordinance, and that if they didn't stop immediately, he would call the sheriff. As anticipated, the other neighbors told him to fuck off. There were more childish insults lobbed before Luther walked back to his house. When a sheriff deputy finally showed up, the fireworks were long gone. The cop said that he could probably could cite a couple of the neighbors for public intoxication but if everybody just moved the party inside, he would forget about it.

Before the deputy could get into his car, Luther came storming from his house. He was furious, you could see it in his face. He screamed at the lawman demanding to know why more deputies hadn't shown up. Why weren't the neighbors being arrested? Was he just going to leave without doing anything? The cop had to threaten Luther with disorderly conduct before he shut up and went back to his house.

The whole incident seemed to hit Luther pretty hard. I'm sure he was already stressed about how the quarantine was affecting his business, but that night must have snapped something else inside of him. One neighbor sent me a screenshot of Luther's Facebook account. He posted this long diatribe about how the police weren't protecting us from lawlessness, and if they wouldn't do it, then he would. He repeated the phrase, "we must unite for law and order." He spent much of the day sitting on his front porch, positioning an AR-15 rifle against the wall to make sure it was visible. He didn't slouch in his chair, his back straight and chest out. When he walked around the neighborhood, he kept his hand close to his waist. He made it no secret on the block that he had his conceal and carry permit.

A forest fire was burning in the state, and the sunsets were beautiful because of the smoke, so I went to the park for a better view. Luther was at the picnic table berating the boy with the long brown hair, and the girl that was usually on the swing. He demanded that they produce identification to prove they lived nearby. I think I have a pretty high tolerance level, but there was no way I was going to let this slide. "Luther, what the fuck are you doing?" I yelled from across the playground. "You leave those kids alone right now"

He looked startled at my voice, "I'm trying to find out if these two are homeless, so we can get them to go somewhere else"

"Did they ask you for help?"

"Michael, if these kids are homeless, they need to be out of this area. There are other resources for these type of people"

"Luther you fucking asshole, these are kids, you leave them alone, or as an attorney I will personally help these two young people file a complaint against you for harassment. I will help them pursue any recourse against you whether its criminal, or civil or both"

He glared at me with his teeth clenched and his right hand in a fist, he was shaking noticeably, "if you start letting homeless people into the park, all the vermin comes with it. The plague will bring it's chaos with it, if......."

"Luther, the two kids are going to own your home when I file a lawsuit against you on their behalf"

He waited until he got to his fence before calling back as loud as he could, "you fucking lawyers have been ruining America for decades. That will be changing"

I asked the kids if they were alright. The girl nodded her head, the boy asked, "What the fuck is wrong with that guy?"

"Some neighbors think he fell on his head too much as a kid, I just think he's an asshole"

I told the kids that I would go get them some food if they were hungry. We ended up eating McDonald's at the picnic table where the boy spent most of his days. My level of anger was growing as Luther watched over the fence, occasionally making it clear that he had his assault rifle close to him. I asked the kids if they had a place to stay, or if there was somebody that I could get in touch with to help them.

The girl said that their dad died last year in a motorcycle accident, and that their mom had been taking care of them, but when the pandemic and quarantine hit, she had to close her hair salon. She used the loan from the government to go buy meth in June, and neither of the kids had seen her since, just a few sporadic phone calls. The boy told me that they were staying at their grandma's house a few blocks from the park, but her and her boyfriend were always drunk and fighting. It was just more peaceful to stay in the park. All of their friends lived across town, and they didn't know anybody here.

"Do you sleep in the park?" I asked them.

"Sometimes. It depends on how drunk they are," the boy said.

"Does anybody bother you?"

"The cops came and talked to me," said the girl, "but when they took me home, my grandma said that I lived there, so the cops just told me I had to be out of the park by ten at night"

"I'm thinking about going and staying at the park in my old neighborhood," the boy told me.

"Why is that?" I asked.

"There's a lot of people that live in that park. Most of them have tents, that's just their home now. Nobody hassles them, because everybody knows how fucked up the world is right now, and that times are hard"

"You would rather stay in a tent in a park, than at your grandma's house?" I asked him.

"Most of the time, yeah"

"What about you?" I asked the girl.

"I like this park. There aren't any bullies here. Most of the time I'm the only one here. I don't mind staying at my grandma's. She barely knows if I'm there or not"

They thanked me for the meal. I pointed to my gate and told them that if they need anything, just come by and ask. The girl went to the swing set, and the boy propped is head on his backpack at the base of a tree. Luther made hard eye contact with me as I walked back to my house. Before I walked in the gate, he held his AR-15 in the air.

That afternoon I drove to all of the Walmart's and Target's and bought all of the tents that were on the shelf. There had been a run on them when the government lockdown began. They were hard to come by. I also bought several sleeping bags. I had to make a second trip in my truck to pick up water and food. I wanted to buy hand sanitizer, but the stores would only sell one at a time.

I went for my usual early morning walk. I didn't see the girl, but the boy was eating something down by the pond. I told him to stop by my place when he was done. When he got there, I gave him a tent, and two sleeping bags. "If you're going to be outdoors," I said to him, "you're going to need some shelter"

"I don't know if I'm going to the park in my old neighborhood. I don't think I should leave my sister. She's to young to be around some the perverts that live there"

"That's why I got the second sleeping bag, in case she wants to stay with you in the park"

"This park?" The boy laughed out loud.

"Yeah, this park"

"You are fuckin' crazy man. You should see the looks that I get from the dogwalkers just for sitting here. These rich mother fuckers would freak the fuck out if they saw a tent in the park"

"Go set up the tent. It's a public park, you have just as much of a right to it as anybody else. If anybody says anything to you, you tell them that I am your attorney and all issues should be addressed with me"

I watched from my back deck as the boy set up the tent in a shaded area near the creek. Luther was watching from his deck too, intermittingly looking over at me with a scowl. I looked at the backyards of other houses that backed up to the park. There were other people around watching the tent be erected. As soon as I saw Luther walking down his stairs, I started walking down mine.

By the time I got there, Luther was standing about ten feet from where the tent was set up and he was on his phone with the sheriff department. When he hung up, I asked Luther if there was a problem.

"Yes, there's a goddamn problem. This is a family park, with children and old ladies. We can't have homeless pieces of shit bring their crime and disease near our homes"

"Jesus fuck Luther. What the fuck is wrong with you? He's a kid"

"Then there should be resources for him, or facilities they can lock him in"

As the deputies approached, I went and handed them my card and introduced myself to them. I explained that I was legal counsel for the boy, and that he was in the process of being emancipated (a lie, but that's how I make a living) and that I had filed a request for a temporary injunction against enforcing the rule that the park close at 10pm (the truth), and therefore the boy was well within his rights to be in his tent in the park. The cops talked on their radios for a few minutes, and then he told Luther that I was right, and there was nothing that could be done until a hearing on the injunction took place next week. I thought a vein in Luther's temple was going to explode as I smiled at him.

Luther adjusted a light in his backyard so that it was directed at the tent. It wasn't bright enough to bother the boy, and it allowed me to keep an eye on the tent. I could hear Luther screaming in his house, and it sounded like his daughters were crying. The next morning on my walk, I saw the boy and asked if he had any trouble during the night. He said he kept hearing noises coming from Luther's but that was it. I asked him if there were any other homeless living in the area. He said that there were a few. I told the boy to tell the others I had tents and sleeping bags if they needed them.

That evening there were four tents pitched in the park. I went to Taco Bell and bought 24 burritos to pass around to the urban campers. Luther once again called the police, and once again I went to the park with paperwork letting them know that the people in the tents could stay there until a hearing was held whether to make the injunction I filed permanent or not. Again, the deputies told him there was nothing that they could do.

The next morning there was a note on my door, not signed, that was in essence a veiled death threat, telling me that I had better watch my back. As I was driving out of the neighborhood, I saw Luther going house to house, taping some kind of flyer to the door. By the third night there were eight tents in the park. They were all young people; the oldest girl might have been 25. I bought them Kentucky Fried Chicken that night. I sat around and talked to them for a while, they were all very respectful and polite. As I excused myself to go home, I noticed that there were no other people in the park, none of my neighbors were in their backyard watching. Luther's light wasn't on. It all seemed so odd.

I had fallen asleep on the couch until I heard the banging at the back door, it was loud and continuous, when I opened the door, it was the boy and he looked panicked. "Call the cops, they're trying to kill us"

"Who?" I brought him in the house and closed the door.

"Some guys, four or five of them, they had machete's and were hacking up the tents. I think they may have set one on fire as I was running here"

When I got to the camp, the one tent that was on fire had burned itself out. I could hear a girl crying somewhere in the dark. A voice from somewhere said that the girl's leg had been burned when she tried to get out of the tent. In seconds, there were sirens and flashing lights everywhere. Other than the guys from the ambulance trying to find the burned girl, none of the other first responders moved with any kind of urgency, some of them never even got out of their car. The firemen used an extinguisher to put out the embers of the tent then left. The cops were just standing around. I walked over to the guy that looked like he was the one that was in charge and identified myself. "Oh, you're the attorney that filed to keep the park open"

"Michael Spinuzzi," I extended my hand.

His arm didn't move. "What can I do for you?"

"As the attorney for these victims, I demand to know what is being done to find these assailants"

"Do live around here Mr. Spinuzzi?"

I pointed, "yeah, over there"

"The cop pointed in the opposite direction; I live in that house over there"

"I fail to see what that has to do with what happened to the people in the tents"

The cop ignored me, "I have two kids, a son who is five, and a daughter who is one. My wife likes to bring them to this park to play"

"I don't think I'm quite following you deputy"

The cop lowered his voice, "you live here too. We can't have this, the neighborhood can't have this"

"So, you're not going to do anything?"

"Well, from what we gathered so far, it sounds like some law-abiding citizens were just trying defend themselves from the vagrants in the tents"

"That's bullshit, and you know it"

"We'll ask around the neighborhood in the morning. Goodnight"

The next morning the boy told me that his mom was trying to get an apartment, and the girl and him would move in there. He thanked me for everything and told me that he would stay in touch. There were several people in the park with clipboards, and others going door to door, asking for signatures to a petition to be presented at the injunction hearing to keep the park closed at ten, and a strict no camping rule.

Finally, and the people rejoiced, the equity in their homes would not be jeopardized by two kids that didn't like staying with their drunken grandma.

Naming My Tumors

I told the hospice nurse to keep the room as dark as possible. She told me that there needed to be at least a little light in the room. I asked her if we could keep it to just the little reading lamp in the corner of my bedroom. She said that would be fine. I thanked her and told her that I just wanted to see if it was true that you see a tunnel of light before you die. She smiled and pushed my hair out of my eyes.

The pain medication did strange things to me. Which I guess is its singular purpose. It's designed to take the mind other places than focusing on the pain. I don't even know if I was in pain or not. Ever since I was diagnosed about nine months ago, I don't recall many episodes of pain.

I've been in my bed for two weeks now. The doctor said I should have died a week ago. I don't know what it is that I am hanging on for. I'm not even sure that I am consciously trying to stay alive. When the doctors told me that it was cancer, I wanted this existence to be over with as soon as possible. That is why I refused to do chemotherapy or any other type of treatment. I've had a life, I won't label it as good, and I won't label it as bad. It was a life, plain and simple.

I haven't had many visitors in the past nine months, but I didn't tell too many people about the diagnoses. Even if I had told everybody in the world, I suspect that I wouldn't have had that many more visitors. My daughter flew out from San Diego when I told her the doctors said there was only a week left. We spent a couple of days together. We laughed, we cried, and we said our goodbyes. She couldn't be away from home long. She has a husband, and two babies under three that needed her.

That's why I was surprised to see her sitting next to my bed when I woke up on Sunday morning. "You should be home with your babies Tarah, but boy, it's good to see you."

She hugged me and kissed me on the forehead. "Tony's mom drove down from Ventura yesterday. She bought me a plane ticket here and told me that she could take care of the babies as long as I needed her to. How are you?"

"The drugs are good. Maybe too good. I think I might just keep hanging around because I like being higher than shit all day. How are Nichole and Justin?"

"Justin is full on into his terrible two's and I can't take an eye off of Nichole or she'll be into everything."

"I hated when you were that age. I was always nervous that we hadn't baby-proofed the house well enough and that you would get hurt."

The nurse came in and asked if I needed anything. "Maybe some coffee and toast. Oh, and a small amount of Diluaded."

"Of course, Alan, I'll check with the doctor and be back shortly," the nurse said.

I just stared at Tarah. "The only hard part of having these tumors all over my body, is that when the grudges finally consume me, I'll have to leave you."

My daughter looked at me suspiciously. "What do you mean, 'when the grudges consume you?"

"I think what cancer is, is grudges that I have held onto in my mind that have manifested themselves into physical poison in my body."

"There might be a little bit more to it than that. You did smoke a lot of cigarettes," she said.

"Sure, there is what the scientists say causes cancer. Religious people think they know what causes cancer. Both sides think they know how to cure it, but when I am laying here in the night, and I can concentrate on my body, my physical shell, I know what caused it and it's not something that will ever show up on an X-ray. I think the only medical person that could have detected my cancer early on, if he knew what he was looking for, would have been a psychiatrist."

"That's an interesting way of looking at it dad."

"I've even given them names."

"Names?" I could hear the skepticism in Tarah's voice.

"Yeah. Names."

"What are they?"

"I think the smallest one is in my thyroid. I named it Karl, after my dad."

"Why would you be holding a grudge against your dad. He died when you were so young. It was a heart attack. He had no control over it."

"I know. It's a small grudge that I have held onto since I was a boy. I just resented him for leaving me when I was so little. There was so much I wanted to do with him. All of the things a boy wants to do with his father. Camping and fishing. Football games. Seeing you being born. There was just so much that he missed out on in my life."

Tarah just stared at me with a look of sympathy on her face.

"There's a tumor in my bladder," I said. "Do you want to know who I named that after?"

"Who?"

"Vanessa."

"Who's that?"

"You were probably too young to remember her. I met her right after I divorced your mom, when you were a baby."

"I don't remember you talking about her."

"I probably never did with you. I was in such pain after your mom and I went our separate ways. Our little family, the three of us, it was all gone."

"Dad, as I've gotten older, and now have a family of my own. I think I understand what happened."

"Thank you, but I wonder if things would have turned out differently if I had never met Vanessa. She blinded me. Of course, I was drinking pretty heavily after the divorce, so my lack of vision might have been self-imposed."

"We all make mistakes dad."

"I know, but I always seemed to compound my own. I don't know what ever happened to Vanessa. She seemed to have just dropped off of the face of the Earth. She changed my life. I really thought I loved her. I thought she was going to fill the void in my life created when I nuked our family, but the opposite was true."

"I have never blamed you for the divorce dad. Maybe when I was younger, just because that's what mom told me, but with age comes wisdom and clarity."

"Maybe your mom and I were just having a rough patch. Maybe we could have found a way to put it all back together, but once I met Vanessa, it was over. I was so in love with...... No, no, no, that isn't right. I was so in lust with her. She was young. She was hot. She could drink just as much as I did, but the real attraction, she loved to fuck, damn, did she like to fuck, anywhere, any time."

"Okay dad, that's enough, this isn't something I really want to talk to you about."

"I'm sorry, that was out of line. Anyway, she never cared about me. She just drained what little money I had. She was a user. Common sense tells me that she had nothing to do with the fracture of our family. I resented her for it. That was a hard grudge to carry."

Tarah didn't say anything. She just raised her eyebrows a little bit. It was an awkward silence. I tried to break it, "see this tube going into my arm?"

She nodded.

"That's how they feed me for the most part. I might be able to eat a little bit of the toast the nurse is bringing me, but only a bite or two. That's all the tumor in my stomach will allow."

"Dad..."

"Tarah, it's important that I say this. I named that tumor Julian."

"Okay."

"I don't know why I actually hold a grudge against Julian, in fact I should feel a sense of gratitude towards him."

"I don't know who Julian is either, dad."

"He was on old drinking buddy back in the day. When the bar would close down, we always go back to my place and keep partying until dawn. He was always the first one there, and the last one to leave. Sometimes he slept on my couch all day. It was kind of pain in the ass, but really, I didn't mind. One night, he didn't come over but I didn't think too much of it. He had been pretty hammered at the bar, so I figured he tapped out. He lived in the same apartment complex as I did. Vanessa lived there too."

"The one in Lakewood?"

"Yeah. Anyway, the night that he wasn't there, I got a cryptic phone call around 3:30 in the morning. It was a voice that I didn't recognize. It just said, 'you need to go check on Julian', and hung up. He had been doing a lot of coke that night. A revolving door in and out of the men's room. The voice on the phone made me worry about that, so I walked over to his apartment. I was afraid of what I might find."

"Was he okay?"

"Oh yeah, more than okay. Through a crack in the curtains, I could see his ass bobbing up and down between a pair of legs. 'Good for him', I thought to myself. I watched for a little while, not being a pervert, but just enjoying the show...."

"That sounds a little perverted to me dad."

"Yeah, I guess it was. I was just kind of laughing about it, until I realized that it was Vanessa's legs he was in between. My stomach just burned. I thought I was going to throw up."

I looked at Tarah. She may have been uncomfortable with the conversation, but she didn't say anything, so I continued. "It was him actually fucking her that made me hold a grudge against him. I knew who she was. Hell, if he would have told me that was what he was going to do, I doubt that I would have even batted an eye. That's just how things were back in the day. It was the betrayal that caused me to hold a grudge, when like I said, it should have been a debt of gratitude. Oh well, enough of that."

The nurse brought in the toast and the coffee and set it on the nightstand. She said she was still waiting for a call back from the doctor about the pain medication. I thanked her and she left the room."

"Hey Tarah?"

"Yes dad."

"I got a funny name for the tumor on my jaw."

"Oh yeah, what is it?"

"Fat Freddie."

"Why Fat Freddie?"

"He was a teacher when I was a sophomore in high school, not one of my teachers, but a teacher. He was also coach of the wrestling team."

"I didn't know you wrestled in high school."

"I didn't."

"So why do you have a grudge against him?"

"For a brief period, when I was young, I chewed tobacco. Skoal."

Tarah cringed a little bit. "Ewww dad, that's really gross."

"I know, but I would have some in my lip in the morning, but would spit it out before I went into the school. One morning I was brushing my hair. In the sink below the mirror I was using, somebody else had spit their tobacco out and not rinsed it down the drain. So Fat Freddie walks in and sees the spit in the sink. He demands that I pull down my lower lip. To make a long story short, there were still flakes in my teeth from the chew I spit out before school. I pleaded that what was in the sink was not mine, but I still ended up getting suspended. Grandma grounded me for two weeks. It may sound silly to you, but that was a bitter grudge I held until I graduated."

"I don't think that's silly at all, Tarah said. "It would piss me off to be accused of something that I didn't do."

"I was pissed off. It changed the way I looked at things. Whenever I heard or read about somebody accused of a crime, I always gave them the benefit of the doubt until a verdict came in."

"That is one thing you taught me dad, and that is to always keep an open mind."

"I don't know if I should tell you what I named the tumor in my lung."

"You don't have to."

"It's Joyce."

"After mom?"

"Yep."

"You don't have to explain that one to me. I'm surprised you only named one after her. She gave you infinite reasons to hold grudges. I have my own grudges against her."

"I won't go into details then, just let me tell you why I named the one in my lung after her. It's because she took my breath away. Twice. The first time was when I first met her. She was so beautiful. So sexy. So much fun to be around. I was so in awe of her, I couldn't breathe. The second time was when we split up. She was gone. I wouldn't be able to see you every day. I couldn't breathe then either, but it was because I thought I was going to die."

"I know dad, but if it's any consolation, I really believe you did the right thing."

"I named the spot on my brain Katherine."

"After Grandma. Why? She is one of the sweetest women I have ever met."

"Yes, she is. The grudge I've held against her is probably more of a post-traumatic stress disorder thing. A little part of me always blamed her for my dad dying. It's stupid. It's irrational. I know it's not the truth, but I can't get it out of my brain. Maybe some of it was because she married Dale so soon after my dad died."

"Dad, I never met your dad, so Dale was who I considered to be my grandpa. I know for fact that he made grandma so happy."

"Yes, he did. That stupid grudge defies all reasoning. I just resented having my life turned upside down so quickly. I readily admit that it is a stupid, selfish grudge. I wish I could deny that it ever existed, but I would only be lying to myself."

"Dad, can I ask you a question?"

"Sure. You can ask me anything."

"How do you know you have all of these tumors? You haven't let the doctor's fully check you out."

"I can feel them. It's like being in a crowd. I don't know anybody around me, but I still know they are there."

"If you say so."

"There are still two tumors that I haven't told you about."

"The first one's name is name is Kristin. It's on my pancreas. Ultimately, that's the one that will probably kill me. That is one mean, evil tumor."

"Why in the hell would name a tumor, I mean hold a grudge against her? When you were married to her is, I think the happiest that I have ever seen you. When I was little, I didn't think you would ever get married again, then she came into your life and you were a different man. Always smiling, always optimistic. I'm shocked that you would hold any kind of grudge against her."

"I shouldn't. Her tumors got the better of her too. She would never have been able to name hers. There were too many of them, millions of them, floating through her blood."

"Your grudge should be against the tumors."

"Tarah, you are trying to argue logic with a dying man. I don't envy you. I guess I think of those tumors as being Kristin. No logic at all. My grudge is that I was robbed of my future, my old age, in just a few short months."

"Don't be offended dad, but that is one of the stupidest things that I have ever heard you say."

"It really is, isn't it? Oh well."

"What's the last one's name?"

I just stared and Tarah, and didn't say a thing. I was regretting ever mentioning it.

"What is it?" She persisted.

"Alan."

I saw the bewilderment on Tarah's face. Her words were measured. "You named a tumor after yourself?"

"Yes. It's on my liver."

"That doesn't even make sense to me."

"It should."

"Why?"

"I think the biggest grudge any person should hold, that is, if they are dumb enough to hold grudges in the first place, is the grudge they hold against themselves."

"I'm not sure I understand what you mean?"

"The first tumor I was diagnosed with was on my liver. That was no accident. That was the result of the life that I have lived. How often have you seen me sober in your life?"

Tarah shrugged her shoulders. "There have been a few times." I think she was trying to make me feel better.

"I hold a grudge against myself because I wasn't a better man."

"You were a great dad."

"Maybe, but I wasn't always a good man. I've been petty. I've been vindictive. My thoughts have crippled me at times. All of the negative thoughts that I have dwelt on in my life. The thoughts that I can temporarily drink away, but they just come back when I'm sober. I hold a grudge against myself for letting those thoughts in. I hold a grudge because there so many good and productive things that I could have focused on in my life."

As Tarah squeezed my hand, the nurse walked in with a syringe. She said that the doctor okayed the pain medication.

As the plunger pushed the drugs into my veins, tears welled up in my eyes as I said to Tarah, "please don't be like me."

Unblemished Sky

The sky was unblemished, there wasn't a cloud in it. There were no trails from airplanes. No birds were flying through it. There was no smoke from the fires even though they are burning just a few miles away. The sky was a deep shade of blue, it almost looked unnatural. The sun had a rosy hue to it.

It was mid-September, but there wasn't a fleck of gold in the trees. The leaves were just as green as they had been in May. Cars lined the street for the baseball game in the park. I watched a kid hit a baseball thrown by the pitcher, but there was no ping that usually accompanied an aluminum bat connecting with the ball. Parents stood around the field with their arms in the air, but I couldn't hear the cheering.

The air was heavy and still, but there was activity all around me. I had a slight ringing in my ears, but all I could hear was the wind gently blowing. I said hello to people I passed on the path, but they kept their eyes elsewhere. I don't think they were ignoring me, because it seemed like they didn't even notice me. I looked down at my feet to make sure they were there because I couldn't feel them making contact with the concrete.

Eventually, I followed a path that I hadn't noticed before. There was a creek running next to it, with only a trickle of water flowing. The path crossed over a short cobblestone bridge. On the other side, there was a surge of electricity that ran through my body. The sun over my shoulder lost its previous hue, in exchange for a shade of crimson red. When I looked at my feet this time, they weren't connecting to the ground"

At the end of the path was a giant weeping willow tree that looked out of place among the firs, pines and aspens. As I got closer, the other trees seemed to go out of focus, while the willow's illumination from the sun brightened against the deep blue background of the sky. There was symphonic hum coming from somewhere. A V-shaped, black alabaster bench sat at the trunk under the crying branches.

I turned and looked at the sound of footsteps coming over the bridge. Against the red sunlight, I could see a black silhouette coming towards me, I recognized the shape. She was a ghost from a long time ago. As she sat down on the bench, she flashed me that sly smile, and had the twinkle of love in her green eyes. From the day that I met her, I wondered if she might be the same woman who inspired Michelangelo's "Mona Lisa". Her face didn't look the same as the last time that she came to me, but I knew it was her. "So, it took you long enough, but you finally made it across the bridge"

I walked over and sat down on the opposite ting of the V. I looked at the way from which I had come, the bridge had crumbled, and water level in the creek was rising. I looked up at the branches above me, and then into her eyes. "I always knew that you would pick a weeping willow tree"

She grabbed a low hanging branch and ran it gently over her lips. "It's beautiful, isn't it?"

"Indeed. It's always a pleasure when I get to see you"

"And you as well." She leaned over and gave me a kiss on the cheek.

"Do you remember when we would be in bed sleeping, in the middle of the night, you'd sit straight up. You'd be shaking, and out of breath..."

"Vividly," she smiled.

"I would ask you if you were alright, and you would grab my arm with both hands, like I'm pulling you up a cliff, and you would say that you were okay, it was just a dream"

"I had some magical dreams when I was there with you"

"You would say that it felt like you had lived a thousand lives in one night. You really did, didn't you?"

"I love you. I love you like no other. That place we were in, trying to be something we're not and never will be, it was good to be in the same time with you, but it was claustrophobic for me. I had to take a holiday to other places"

"I loved those times, but I knew they would be fleeting. I knew you couldn't be captured"

"You are so silly. In the place you live, I've only been gone seven years in the way time is measured there. That's not even a trillionth of a nanosecond in the entirety of it all"

"I just wish that you would have warned me a little sooner. We could have made some other type of arrangement"

"We did. That's why I'm here now"

"It killed me when you left. I've been lost without you"

She laughed, and shook her head in mild disgust, "I never left you, and you know it, you're just feeling sorry for yourself, and it's not terribly attractive. I merely stepped into another room"

"I held your hand as you took your last breath, I watched you die"

"There is no such thing as death, it's just an illusion to help you understand this process," she held up her hands to the tree, "all of this, what you think is reality, is just a great big party. There are infinite rooms with guests in all of them, it's important to get out and mingle. As before, and as we have done many times in the past, we are once again in the same room"

I looked over at the bridge as the water swept part of it away, "Am I dead?"

She put her hand to her forehead in frustration, "I just told you that there is no such thing as a death. That's was one of your faults when we were together, you wouldn't listen. You know what is happening, you're just being stubborn"

"Why now?'

She stood up from the bench and grabbed my hand, "let's walk". She pushed through a jumble of branches revealing a path of red dirt cutting through a golden valley of weeping willow trees rising out an endless field of wheat. "The only time was now"

"What happened to me?"

"It wasn't just you. It was everybody. They're all in their own little rooms now with someone who is to them as I am to you"

"My daughter?"

"She's fine. She's in a similar place to you right now. You'll find her soon, once you remember how this station works"

"My friends? My fami...."

"Everybody." She squeezed my hand as we walked. "It's all gone"

I looked back to the path being overgrown by the wheat, "tell me what happened"

"I'm honestly surprised you can't figure that out for yourself," her tone laced with sarcasm. "You spent 55 years there, you had to have seen the writing on the wall"

"I'm remembering it now. I volunteered to go there. I was warned that it would be a dangerous and risky existence"

"I tried to talk you out of it. You pleaded with me to go with you. We were perfectly contented where we were. It's just your nature to never be satisfied"

"I knew it was a new prototype, an entirely different type of existence. EARTH. Do you remember what the acronym stood for?"

"Experimental....something or rather," she couldn't think of it.

"You still really haven't said what happened. I just remember walking in the park. There was a girl on the swings, and boy setting up a tent. Then I took a path that I had never noticed before. That's all I remember"

"You were in a coma"

"I don't know what you're talking about"

"What did you do the last six months?"

"Well, not much of anything. There was a virus, there was nothing we could do. They wouldn't let us travel too far from home. They took all of our money. The grocery store shelves were empty. There were fires everywhere"

"That was part of the virus, they made it up in labs. It had cell-sized microchips in it, so that the humans could be controlled. It didn't work the way it was supposed to. Everybody who volunteered for that existence was supposed to have been extracted immediately"

"I don't understand"

"Those last six months, were they like any you had experienced before?"

"No"

"It was determined that EARTH was too far of a dangerous experiment to continue. Some say it was because of the humans, but the place deteriorated far faster than was expected. There virus extraction was supposed to be instantaneous, the blink of an eye. Something went wrong. You were all to be put to sleep until the problem was figured out. Those last six months had to have been terrifying. They had to implant a contrived reality for you. It was the only way to free you"

"Where is this path going?"

"Where you've always wanted to be"

www.ingramcontent.com/pod-product-compliance
Lightning Source LLC
Chambersburg PA
CBHW051417170626
46809CB00006B/2203